Privy to Injury

Slocum's horse was in sight, but his gun was hanging on the wall behind the sheriff. In the few seconds it took for him to think about that, he heard a grunt from the outhouse. Lyle, the young deputy, pulled the door open and stepped outside before Slocum could find a place to hide.

Slocum grabbed the young man's shirt in both hands and hauled him into the open, ramming straight into him with an outstretched arm that caught the deputy squarely between the neck and shoulders. Lyle practically folded. To his credit, he managed to pull his pistol from its holster before Slocum could stop him. Even so, Lyle wasn't fast enough to fire a shot before Slocum's boot pinned the man's gun hand against the dirt.

"You're gonna make plenty of noise when you pull that trigger. After that, the sheriff will come out here and blast you in half."

"If I'd wanted you dead, I would have shot you up close without making much noise at all," Slocum said.

JAKE LOGAN

SLOCUM
AND THE
LIVING DEAD MAN

JOVE BOOKS, NEW YORK

THE BERKLEY PUBLISHING GROUP
Published by the Penguin Group
Penguin Group (USA) Inc.
375 Hudson Street, New York, New York 10014, USA
Penguin Group (Canada), 90 Eglinton Avenue East, Suite 700, Toronto, Ontario M4P 2Y3, Canada
(a division of Pearson Penguin Canada Inc.)
Penguin Books Ltd., 80 Strand, London WC2R 0RL, England
Penguin Group Ireland, 25 St. Stephen's Green, Dublin 2, Ireland (a division of Penguin Books Ltd.)
Penguin Group (Australia), 250 Camberwell Road, Camberwell, Victoria 3124, Australia
(a division of Pearson Australia Group Pty. Ltd.)
Penguin Books India Pvt. Ltd., 11 Community Centre, Panchsheel Park, New Delhi—110 017, India
Penguin Group (NZ), 67 Apollo Drive, Rosedale, North Shore 0632, New Zealand
(a division of Pearson New Zealand Ltd.)
Penguin Books (South Africa) (Pty.) Ltd., 24 Sturdee Avenue, Rosebank, Johannesburg 2196,
South Africa

Penguin Books Ltd., Registered Offices: 80 Strand, London WC2R 0RL, England

This is a work of fiction. Names, characters, places, and incidents either are the product of the author's imagination or are used fictitiously, and any resemblance to actual persons, living or dead, business establishments, events, or locales is entirely coincidental.

SLOCUM AND THE LIVING DEAD MAN

A Jove Book / published by arrangement with the author

PRINTING HISTORY
Jove edition / November 2009

1

McKalb, Montana Territory

No guns allowed within town limits.

At least, that's what the sign outside of McKalb said. Enforcing that decree was a whole other problem.

John Slocum wasn't the kind of man who broke the law whenever it suited him, but he also wasn't the sort who was willing to hand over his six-shooter just because a weather-beaten piece of lumber told him to. There were too many snakes along the trail to pose a problem for a man riding on his own. From Slocum's experience, he knew the truly bothersome snakes were the ones who walked on two legs and liked to shoot at unsuspecting backs.

Slocum had been riding for the better part of a week and was enjoying every last second of it. The Montana Territory unfolded like a picture book to show him something new every day. Flat prairies gave way to rolling hills, and then those hills swelled up into distant mountain ranges. All the while, the vast expanse of blue stretched out overhead to make good on all the promises implied by the term "Big Sky Country." Slocum probably could have made it to McKalb much quicker, but he'd taken his time to soak up as much as he could. Besides, there was no reason to rush. Nellie Sayers would wait for him.

The last time he'd crossed paths with Nellie, she'd been pulling her money together to get her own hotel off the ground. Being one of her investors back when she'd been scrambling for funds, Slocum kept in touch with Nellie as much as time and the post office would allow. The letters he occasionally got from her had been as good as could be expected from someone starting up a business. Even more promising were the assurances that Slocum's investment could be repaid at any time. Nellie had asked for an address to send him the money, but Slocum always insisted she should keep it for just a little while longer. The truth of the matter was that he looked forward to collecting it in person.

McKalb was on the eastern end of the Montana Territory, and Slocum rode in while the sun was on its way down to meet the western horizon. The gray stallion he'd bought from a dealer in Cody, Wyoming, had proven to be sturdy enough, but hadn't been put up in a proper stable for some time. The strong fella didn't fret, however, and galloped past the battered antigun notice with plenty of steam in his strides.

Slocum's Colt Navy hung at his side like an extension of his body. Its weight was familiar on his hip, and he didn't even think about steering toward the closest lawman before heading for the first suitable stable that caught his eye. After all, the stallion had done a hell of a lot more for Slocum than any lawman who didn't even have the gumption to maintain a sign.

The main street was just wide enough for a wagon and horse to pass each other, and ran more or less straight through town. A few smaller roads branched off from that one, with several crooked alleys leading to lots and such behind the most prominent rows of storefronts. The stable Slocum had spotted was about a quarter of the way down the street on the right-hand side. Inside, the place was dry despite the previous night's rain, and the air smelled like fresh hay. Those things, along with the eager little girl in coveralls who ran out to greet him, were all pretty good signs.

"Take your horse, mister?" the little girl asked.

Slocum couldn't help but grin down at her. Before he could answer her question, a stout fellow with a long silver beard came out to collect the girl. "Don't bother the man, child," the old man scolded.

But the girl would have none of it and started to rush toward Slocum's horse. "I can brush him an' everything, mister. I'll do a fine job!"

The old man might not have been as quick on his feet as the girl, but his hand was fast enough to snap out and grab hold of the back of her coveralls. Nearly lifting her up off her feet, he grumbled, "Beggin' ain't no way to conduct business, Megan Belle. Now git on inside. Yer barely even properly dressed to be out where all can see ya."

Her head wasn't much higher than the old man's waist, but she glared back at him as if she was the one in charge. "I don't need a dress to brush a horse!"

"And you don't need one to clean out them stalls, so get back to it!" Once the little girl was huffing away, the old man turned toward Slocum. "Hope the child didn't get underfoot," he said with a shake of his head. "Just a little anxious, is all."

"She's good enough at drumming up customers," Slocum replied. "Got any room for my horse in there?"

"Sure enough."

"How about the offer for a good brushing? That still on the table?"

Megan snapped her head back to flash Slocum a cute little smile. She didn't say anything, but watched from one of the stalls while the old man chewed on his whiskers.

"She does a good job," the old man said. "But rest assured, I'll go back to make sure of it."

Slocum nodded. "Good enough for me."

That was also plenty good enough for Megan, because she was singing a happy tune while Slocum paid for the next two nights in advance. He left the stable with his saddlebags slung over his shoulder and Megan's song rattling around the back of his head. It was a short enough walk to Nellie's hotel that he arrived before he started whistling the child's tune out loud.

Unfortunately, all he found in the lot he'd helped Nellie pick out the last time he'd been in town was half a set of charred steps and a few blackened walls. The rest of the hotel had obviously gone up in one hell of a blaze.

Slocum stood there gawking at the remains for a minute or two. When it became clear that the scorched hunks of wood weren't about to answer any of his questions, he shifted his bags on his shoulder and moved along. That little surprise took a good portion of the wind from his sails, making him feel as though the saddlebags were growing heavier with every step. The occasional stare he got from a passing local only served to deepen the scowl upon his face. Slocum hauled his tired carcass and heavy saddlebags into the Slippery Rock Saloon just down the street, and was greeted by another disapproving stare.

"You ain't supposed to carry guns in town," announced the young man tending bar.

Slocum dropped his bags and propped one foot on the tarnished brass rail that kept a row of spittoons in line. "Are you the law?"

"No."

"Are you the bartender?"

The man looked to his left and right as though he was searching for an ambush. Deciding the question was just as simple as it sounded, he replied, "Yeah."

"Then give me a drink and let a lawman do the rest."

One of the few other patrons in the place was a gnarled fellow whose scarred face and calloused hands made him seem several decades older than he truly was. "He's got ya there, Larry."

"Yes, but Sheriff White will get me, too, if he sees me serving drinks to an armed man." Shifting his eyes back toward Slocum, Larry added, "And I don't cater to them that's gotta have a pistol handy just to enjoy some of the best whiskey in the territory."

Slocum pulled his Colt Navy from its holster, unloaded it, and let the pistol dangle by one finger stuck through the trigger guard. Pocketing the bullets and setting the gun on the bar, he growled, "That whiskey had better be damn good."

Larry didn't need to be told how attached Slocum was to the six-shooter. He kept his eyes locked on the gun's owner as he carefully took the Colt and moved it to the counter where several green bottles were lined up. Setting the pistol down as if it were a coiled snake, he said, "Right there where you can see it, mister. I just don't wanna be stuck with no more fines, is all."

Slocum nodded and waited for his whiskey to be poured. When the glass in front of him was ready, he lifted it to his mouth and tossed it back. The liquid fire scorched a trail down to his gut, burning away a good amount of trail dust before settling in for the night. When he set the glass down, Slocum nodded and said, "That's pretty good stuff."

"On the house." Noting the raise of Slocum's eyebrow, Larry said, "For bein' understanding about the town policy and all. Lots of fellas put up more of a stink."

"Even better then. Set me up with another."

After the second shot went down, Slocum felt as if he'd taken off a set of blinders. He'd stalked into the Slippery Rock in a foul mood that had come on like a storm. Now that he'd gotten what he was after, Slocum looked around to notice that several tables were occupied by cardplayers and drunks alike. A reed of a man strummed a guitar in the back corner of the place, coaxing a tired smile onto Slocum's face. Of course, the third shot of whiskey also went a long way in that regard.

As if sensing the change in Slocum's mood, Larry sidled up to offer the bottle one more time. Slocum held out his glass, so the barkeep filled it. "You just passing through McKalb?"

"Actually, I was here to visit the Sayers Grand Hotel."

"If someone told you they were stayin' at the Grand, they was lying through their teeth. That place burnt down last spring."

"That's the first I've heard of it."

"Probably because The Wheelhouse is a whole lot better."

"The Wheelhouse?" Slocum asked. "Is that another hotel?"

Larry nodded and leaned with one elbow against the bar. "Not the finest in town, but some folks seem to like it. If you're lookin' for a place to stay, I got a few rooms to rent. Otherwise, you could try the Clarkson Inn at the end of the street."

"So The Wheelhouse just happened to open up when the Grand burnt down?" Gritting his teeth, Slocum added, "That's real interesting."

"Not really. Just a bunch of beds and a passable restaurant under a different roof."

"What about the owner of the Grand? Is she still about?"

Shrugging, Larry finally took notice of one of the gamblers wildly flapping at him to refill the glasses at that table. "From what I hear, that place had plenty of owners. If you want my opinion, ain't no better place than the Clarkson."

Slocum chuckled and held up his glass. "Let me guess. The Clarkson also serves the finest whiskey?"

"Delivered twice weekly from this very establishment." Larry beamed. "Now, if you'll excuse me, I need to tend to these fine gentlemen at a poker game that's known throughout the territory and beyond."

Judging by the showmanship Larry put into his last few sentences, the barkeep not only provided liquor for the Clarkson Inn, but also got a healthy cut of the gambling revenue at the Slippery Rock. It wasn't a bad setup for an enterprising businessman, but didn't exactly make Larry a credible spokesman regarding the town's hotels. Slocum had to admit, however, that the man did have good taste in whiskey. After draining the last of what remained in his glass, Slocum collected his saddlebags and leaned toward a weathered man propped up a bit farther along the bar.

"You know where The Wheelhouse is?" Slocum asked.

"Make a left outta this place, then another at the corner and a right at the next one. Can't miss it."

Considering the modest size of McKalb, those directions were more than enough to suit Slocum's needs. Since Larry was busy talking up the gamblers, he helped himself to his pistol and left the Slippery Rock. He was still fitting the bullets into the Colt's cylinder when he spotted a pair of men staring at him from across the street. Although Slocum couldn't make out any tin pinned to the men's chests, the holsters around their waists led him to believe they were the local law. Either that, or they paid even less attention to the town's ordinances than he did.

Slocum tipped his hat and started walking along the uneven boardwalk. Whether those two men were law or trouble, he guessed he wouldn't have to wait long for them to show their cards. Sure enough, before he walked far enough to make his second left, Slocum heard two sets of heavy footsteps thumping on the boardwalk to catch up to him. He crossed the street, stopped at the corner, and then immediately turned around. The two men following Slocum stopped short in the middle of the street. Neither of them looked to be much more than a year or two into their twenties. One had a poor excuse for a beard sprouting from his chin, and the other had a face that no amount of whiskers could age. Despite looking like an overgrown kid, the clean-shaven man stood tall, while his partner backed up half a step.

"Ordinance says no guns are to be carried in town," the clean-shaven man said.

"And are you the men who enforce the ordinances?" Slocum asked.

"That's right."

"I don't see any proper identification." Smirking at how the other two men chewed on those words, Slocum added,

"No badges. I don't see any badges. For all I know, you could be robbers trying to make me hand over my only form of protection."

That confused the young man with the beard no end. "Robbers? We're deputies. Hand over the damn pistol!"

If the men had announced themselves in a civil tone before stomping after him and tossing about loud demands, Slocum might have been more inclined to go along with them. Although he wasn't about to start any real trouble, he didn't feel like caving in so quickly to the strutting boys. "I'm not just going to hand over my pistol to anyone who asks for it," Slocum said. "That's how things get stolen, you know."

The man with the beard sputtered and started to charge forward, but was stopped by the other one's arm. Holding his partner back, the clean-shaven man said, "You must've seen the sign and we're obviously not robbin' no one."

"Where's your badges?"

"Don't need 'em. Everyone in town knows who we are and they know we work for Sheriff White."

Slocum shrugged. "But I don't know you from Adam. I'll stop by the sheriff's office to comply with the town ordinance as soon as I get settled. If that's not good enough, I'll be at The Wheelhouse Hotel. Maybe someone there can verify who you are."

The bearded man didn't like being put through the wringer, but the clean-shaven one seemed to know it wasn't going to amount to anything serious. Even so, he didn't appreciate the grief. "What's your name, mister?"

"John Slocum. I'd shake your hands, but I'm in a rush." He only added that part to aggravate the bearded man a little more. There was just something about that one that spurred Slocum to be a little more ornery than usual.

"John Slocum, you say?"

Slocum had started walking away, but turned when he heard the clean-shaven man's question. It wasn't uncommon for someone to recognize his name, but that wasn't always a good thing. While some folks might have heard stories about Slocum's deeds, there were plenty out there nursing some very nasty grudges where those same deeds were concerned. "That's right. Have we met?"

The clean-shaven man shook his head. "You'll be at The Wheelhouse then?"

"Right again."

The man with the beard started to spout a threat or some other batch of bold words, but was cut short by a slap from his partner's forearm. After that same partner shot him a look, both of them backed up and moved along.

Slocum stood at the corner, waiting for the two to say or do something else. Instead, they simply walked away while casting the occasional glance in his direction. If they were truly lawmen, they would most likely go crying back to the man who paid their salaries.

The directions Slocum had been given were good enough to get him to within half a block of The Wheelhouse Hotel. Just as he'd been promised, the place was hard to miss.

2

The Wheelhouse was a wide building that smelled like freshly cut pine. Every plank had sharp, new edges and came together to form an impressive structure. Even the sign above the front door was bright and clean, as if it had been painted a few hours prior to Slocum's arrival. Slocum was greeted by a young boy in short pants who hurried out to light the lanterns hanging from a balcony overlooking the street. The kid held the door open for Slocum and then went about his duty.

Inside, the place was just what was advertised. Clean floors were partially covered by new rugs. A few small tables held vases of fresh flowers. And behind the front desk, there stood a woman in her late forties with a freshly scrubbed face and dark blond hair pulled back into a bun. The woman smiled at Slocum, and kept beaming until he walked up to her desk.

"Welcome to The Wheelhouse," she said. "Care for a room or are you just here for dinner?"

"I just wanted a room, but is that dinner I smell right now?"

"Sure is. Our cook made a batch of his famous beef stew and it's been simmering all day long. It's getting a little late for service, but we can make an exception for one of our guests."

"Sold," Slocum told her. "I'll take a room and some of that stew."

"Excellent."

While the clerk scribbled something into her ledger, Slocum asked, "How long has this place been open?"

"A few months."

"And what about the Sayers Grand?"

When he'd asked that question, Slocum had intended on fishing for some bit of information from the clerk's eyes. He'd played more than enough poker to catch a hint of when someone was hiding something or when they were working an angle. All he saw in the woman's eyes was a whole lot of blue.

"It's a right shame what happened to the Grand," she told him. "Still, The Wheelhouse is here now and it's a whole lot better than that old place used to be. Do you prefer to have a room overlooking the street, or would you rather have a view of the outskirts of town?"

"I'd like to watch the street."

She nodded and turned the ledger around so he could sign it. When he was finished, she turned the book around again and had a look. "Glad to have you here, Mr. Slocum. If you're hungry, I can have a boy bring your bags up to your room so you can go right in and have some supper."

Since the kid had returned from lighting the outside lanterns and was eagerly anticipating Slocum's answer, he eased the saddlebags from his shoulder and said, "That sounds good. These bags are kind of heavy, though."

The kid took the bags in both hands and attempted to drape them over his shoulders the way Slocum had done. "These ain't . . . heavy," the boy huffed. After taking a few steps toward the nearby staircase, he added, "Not too heavy for me."

The blonde came out from behind the desk and dropped a key into the boy's shirt pocket. "Room Number Four. You sure you don't need any help?"

"I'm strong enough."

"Is there anything fragile in those bags, Mr. Slocum?" she asked.

"I sure hope not. After all the riding I've done, anything too delicate would be cracked into bits. I'd say that boy has what it takes to climb those stairs."

Inspired by those words, the boy gripped the saddlebags with both hands and quickened his pace.

The blond clerk watched until the boy made it more than halfway up the steps, and then led the way into the next room. "If you come with me, I can see to it that you get seated right away."

Since less than half of the tables in the dining room were full, Slocum knew there wasn't much of a chance of him getting turned away. Still, the blonde was pleasant company. Several long strands of hair had escaped her bun to lay along the smooth contour of her neck. Her skin gave off the scent of rosewater and a bit of perfume. Before he could take in more than that, Slocum found himself at a little square table situated in front of a picture window.

"How about that one over there instead?" he asked while pointing to a table that wouldn't put him on display.

"Whatever you like. Do you already know what you want?"

Slocum let his eyes wander up and down the blonde's curves before meeting her blue eyes and nodding. "I sure do."

She titled her head a bit and grinned to make it clear she knew exactly what he meant. "How about the beef stew?" she offered.

"And what about dessert?"

"You like peach pie?"

"Sure, but perhaps you could recommend something better."

"How about you start there and see what kind of specials tomorrow brings?"

Slocum nodded and placed his napkin upon his lap. "Fair enough. I don't plan on running off."

"Well, now," she replied in a very encouraging tone.

"That's real good to hear." As she turned and walked over to deliver Slocum's order to the kitchen, the clerk shifted her hips in a way that a woman only used when she knew she was being watched. The smirk she wore as she headed back to the front desk told Slocum that she didn't mind him watching in the slightest.

The beef stew was brought out without much of a wait, and was served in a wide, shallow bowl with two biscuits balanced upon the edge. Slocum's stomach growled the instant he caught sight of his food, and he tore into the stew like a condemned man wolfing down his last meal. The chunks of beef fell apart in his mouth, and the biscuits were perfect for sopping up whatever his spoon had left behind. As good as that first helping was, the second was even better. Slocum savored every bite. By the time he was finished, he'd almost forgotten about dessert. A slice of peach pie was delivered to his table without him having to ask for it, accompanied by a cup of coffee.

Hoisting himself from his chair, Slocum paid his bill and went to the front desk.

"How was your supper?" the blonde asked.

"Even better than it smelled and that's saying quite a lot. Thanks for the pie, by the way."

"It was just my suggestion."

"And a good one. How much longer do you have to stand behind that desk?" he asked.

"A while. Someone was asking about you."

"Really? Who?"

"Sheriff White. He sent one of his boys around asking about anyone walking in wearing a gun. There's an ordinance against that, you know."

Slocum did a fairly good job of keeping a straight face when he said, "Is that so? Someone should post a sign."

"I didn't tell them you were eating in the next room, but they know you could be found here," she explained. "I think they might come back."

"I'll go see the sheriff personally as soon as I clean up a

bit. Besides, I'm so full right now that I'll barely make it up the stairs. Getting down the street might be a problem. Since dinner was so good, I'd like to compliment the management. Any chance I might be able to have a word with someone in that regard?"

"You want to speak to the manager?"

"Preferably the owner," Slocum said. "I've got some questions."

The clerk grinned, but tried to cover it up by turning toward the wall behind her and reaching for a key. When she handed the key to Slocum, she barely even met his eyes. "I'll see if I can scrape up the management. Here's the key to your room. It's Number Four."

Slocum took the key and studied the blonde's nervous mannerisms. As a way to test the waters, he let his fingertips graze along hers. Sure enough, he could see the blush on her cheeks no matter how bashful she seemed to be. "Maybe you could show me to my door?"

"I don't think so," she replied. "I'm sure you're tired and just want to get some rest."

"Maybe later then?"

"Sure. I might just take you up on that."

Although he could have thought of a much better outcome to that conversation, the blonde didn't give him anything but encouraging signs. "What's your name?"

"Kate."

"I'll be looking for you, Kate," Slocum promised.

Judging by the smile on her face, Kate wasn't about to make herself too hard to find.

Slocum walked across the lobby and climbed the stairs to the second floor. Each step was too new to squeak and every handle of every door looked as if it had been freshly polished. While he wasn't happy about Nellie's place getting burned down, he had to admit that her competition sure knew how to run a hotel. Now he wanted to make sure the fire that had claimed the Sayers Grand was an accident and not a quick way to thin the herd.

He unlocked his door and pushed it open. In the few seconds it took for the door to swing on its hinges, Slocum spotted two things: his saddlebags resting on the floor and someone waiting for him inside the room. His hand darted to his cross-draw holster and drew the Colt Navy out of pure reflex.

"Nervous, John?"

Slocum stood in the doorway, studying the intruder without truly believing his eyes. "Nellie?"

It was Nellie, all right. She'd been sitting on the edge of his bed, and now stood up. Her skin was the color of lightly creamed coffee and smoother than the silk draped over the bed. Her hair was a thick cascade of tight curls spilling over her shoulders and down her back. Although her curves were a bit more rounded than the last time he'd seen her, the touch of extra weight was in all the right places. Slocum could tell that much because the only thing Nellie wore was a sheet that she'd pulled from the bed to press against her bare breasts.

"What the hell are you doing here?" Slocum asked.

She walked forward, keeping the sheet pressed against her front, which didn't do much to cover her from the waist down. "You want me to leave?" she asked. Before Slocum could answer her, she'd gotten close enough to reach between his legs and cup his stiffening cock. "Oh, my. I think I know just what you want me to do."

Slocum might have been confused, but he wasn't dead. He also wasn't about to force Nellie to stop what she was doing. "How'd you get into my room?"

Nellie stopped and blinked as she looked at him with disbelief. "When did you start asking so many questions? This is my hotel, so I can get into any room I want."

"This is your hotel?"

"Yes. Isn't that why you came?"

"Last time I checked, your hotel was the Sayers Grand," Slocum pointed out.

She chuckled and shook her head. "That place burned

down, but I had enough money stashed to get a fresh start here. In fact, that place was such a success that my investors kicked in some more for me to do the new place up right. What do you think?"

"I think I need to keep up on my correspondence. I came into town to pay you a visit. When I found the cinders of the old place and heard about this new one that cropped up, I came along to have a word with the manager. Sometimes, fires like that aren't an accident."

Nellie stepped up so her breasts grazed Slocum's chest. She brought her hand up to his cheek and cooed, "You meant to scare the hell out of someone who might've chased me out of business? That's sweet. Still, I can fend for myself just fine."

"I'll say. How did you know I was here? My visit was supposed to be a surprise."

"It almost was," she said. "I just happened to see your name on the register when making my rounds, so I slipped up here to give you a proper greeting."

When he looked back on it now, Slocum could see why Kate had been giggling so much after supper. It was mighty difficult to think about her or any other woman when Nellie was so close. He was even further distracted when she let her sheet drop so she could place both hands on his face and pull him down for a kiss.

"My protector," she whispered.

"Protecting you from nothing," he pointed out.

She kept kissing him. In between kisses, she said, "My favorite investor then."

Slocum placed his hands on her hips and pulled her close. "That'll do." With that, he slid a hand up along her back until he reached the back of her head. That way, he could wrap her up and hold her tight as he kissed her long and deep.

Nellie stood on her toes and rubbed her leg up and down Slocum's hip. When he reached around to cup her generous backside in both hands, she crawled up to wrap both legs around his waist and lock her hands behind his neck. Slocum was completely enveloped by her sweet, womanly scent just as he was enveloped by her body. He savored the feel of her soft, rounded body as it wriggled in his hands and ground against his torso. She'd always been a wild lover, but now she seemed damn near possessed.

The instant Slocum carried her to the bed, she hopped down and began pulling at the buttons of his shirt. She barely had that open before shifting her hands to his belt buckle and pants. By the time she'd peeled his jeans down to free his stiffening member, she was pulling him onto the bed.

"Damn," Slocum grunted as he hit the mattress. "You really did miss me."

Climbing down to kneel on the floor at the foot of the bed, she reached for his erection and said, "I meant to do this before you left the last time and I've been thinking about it ever since." As soon as those words were out, she placed her lips upon the tip of his cock and took him all the way into her mouth. When her lips touched the base of his shaft, she grabbed hold of his legs and began bobbing her head up and down vigorously. After a few minutes of that, she looked up with a wide smile on her face, climbed onto the bed, and slowly moved over him.

Her pendulous breasts swayed and she brushed her dark nipples along Slocum's legs. Nellie dug her fingernails into his chest while straddling him and rubbing her moist pussy against the length of his cock. Slocum reached down to fit himself between her legs. The moment his rigid pole eased inside her, she lowered herself onto him and started grinding back and forth.

"Oh, yeah," she moaned. "Even better than I remember."

Slocum didn't say a word. He did his talking with his hands as he grabbed her hips and moved her even faster. When she quickened her pace a little more, Slocum tightened his grip to stop her dead in her tracks. Waiting until she looked down at him, Slocum thrust up into her to send a ripple of excitement through Nellie's entire body. She started to say something, but her words were lost amid a series of breathless grunts as Slocum pounded into her again and again. Finally, she leaned forward and placed her lips against his ear to grunt and groan while he vigorously pumped between her legs.

Every inch of Nellie's body was soft and warm. He slowed his pace a bit while letting his hands wander along the smooth, supple curves of her sides and back. Her breasts overflowed from his hands when he cupped them, and she let out a squeal of pleasure when he rolled her nipples between his thumb and forefinger. Sitting up, Nellie pressed her hands over Slocum's to hold them in place on her breasts. She straightened her back and thrust her hips back and forth, tightening around his cock as if she was never going to let him slip out of her. Eventually, she let go of his hands so she could place hers flat on Slocum's stomach. From there, she locked eyes with him and rocked back and forth.

Nellie rode him vigorously, pinning him to the bed as her throaty moans became louder and louder. When she climaxed, Slocum could feel her entire body trembling until a shuddering breath escaped from the back of her throat. Just when it seemed she was about to collapse, Slocum rolled her onto her side and climbed off the bed.

"It's good to have you back," she sighed. When she reached for the blanket, she felt Slocum's hands guiding her once more.

"Good to be back," Slocum said as he walked to the side of the bed and turned her around so her back was facing him. "But I'm not through with you yet."

As soon as she felt Slocum's hand pushing against her back, she eagerly followed his lead and got on all fours. Her knees were on the edge of the mattress and her hands made fists around the blanket. Feeling his hands on her generous hips, Nellie lowered her shoulders, arched her back, and spread her legs in anticipation of his return. She only had to wait a few seconds before she felt his rock-hard cock ease into her from behind.

Slocum kept his hands on her hips as he thrust in and out.

With him standing against the bed and Nellie positioned on top of it, he entered her at just the right angle to get her moaning again. Just when he'd hit his stride, Slocum leaned forward to grab her shoulders and pull her toward him as he pumped into her. Nellie propped herself up and tossed her hair back while letting out another series of groans.

"That's it!" she moaned. "Right there. Don't stop."

Now it was Slocum's turn to lean back and enjoy himself. He closed his eyes and savored the way her round backside bumped against him as he entered her. Then he watched Nellie claw at the bed like a cat as she rocked in time to his thrusts. Slocum placed one hand at the small of her back and slipped his fingers through her hair. That caused her to stretch her head back as if silently begging him to keep going.

Rather than disappoint her, Slocum grabbed her hair and pulled just enough to force her head back as he drove into her one more time. Rather than continue with the pace he'd set, he buried his cock all the way in and held it there. Nellie didn't waste a moment before grinding back and forth until he was hitting her in just the right spot. She climaxed again, but was too breathless to do more than tremble.

Slocum pulled her hair again and started pumping in and out like a piston. No longer holding himself back, he rubbed her hip with his free hand before giving her ass a sharp little slap. Nellie responded to that with a surprised yelp and growled for him to do it again. Slocum obliged, but slapped her a little harder. When he let go of her hair, she drove her face into the mattress and let out a scream that would have filled the entire upper floor. When she was done with that, she looked back at him and watched him intently.

"Go on, John. Keep at it. Do whatever you want. I'm all yours."

He grabbed her with both hands to rub the curves of her hips and backside as he had his way with her. He could even feel her shake with what could have been another orgasm before he finally felt his own come along. When it surged through him, he gripped Nellie's round ass and pumped into her one more time.

"That's it, baby," she sighed. "Give it all to me."

Slocum blinked as the last bit of energy drained out of him. Keeping inside her, he swiped his hair back and asked, "Do any of your workers know you talk like that?"

"Why do you think I tried so hard to keep my voice down?"

"That was you keeping your voice down?"

"What can I say?" She chuckled. "You bring out the devil in me."

He backed up and allowed Nellie to roll onto her side. She had a trace of a handprint on her backside, which she gingerly rubbed. "Sorry about that," he said.

"No you're not. And neither am I. If I would've known you had that much bottled up in you, I would have tracked you down a long time ago. You know I still owe you a return on your investment, don't you?"

"Taking money from you right now doesn't quite feel right."

"Oh," Nellie said. "Then I can just keep your money for myself."

"Give it to me later. It should feel just fine then."

"Only if you promise to do the same," she playfully replied. Nellie lay on her side, naked as the day she was born and perfectly content to stay that way.

"This is one hell of a nice place," he said as he lay down beside her. "How'd you pull together the money so fast?"

"I told you, the Grand was a success. Even though none of my partners will say as much, they don't mind keeping their noses out of my hotel and letting me build it up. I've only had problems with one investor in particular. Seems he can't be bothered to collect what he's earned. I swear, when I get my hands on that one . . ." Seeing the sly glance Slocum gave her, Nellie laughed and added, "Guess I already did."

Before Slocum could make any comments about the amazing room service at The Wheelhouse, someone knocked on the door. He pulled on his pants, and was getting into his shirt when a meek voice came through the door.

"Excuse me," a woman in the hallway said. "Miss Sayers?"

Nellie sat up and practically flew into a dress that had been piled into a corner. "Is that you, Kate?"

"Yes, ma'am. Sheriff White is downstairs and one of his deputies is out here with me. They'd like to have a word with you about one of the guests."

3

Freezing while sliding her arm through one sleeve, Nellie looked over at Slocum and whispered, "Are you in any sort of trouble?"

"Why would you ask that?" Slocum replied, instinctively matching her hushed tone.

"Because otherwise, she would have just asked me to come out whenever I pulled myself together."

"Does she know what you were doing in here?" Thinking back to the mischievous giggling fit that had overtaken the blond clerk after supper, Slocum added, "Forget I asked that. I'm not on the run from the law, if that's what you mean."

"Don't you have a price on your head?"

"Sure, but not in this neck of the woods. At least, not as far as I can recall."

Suddenly, Nellie glanced at the gun belt lying on the floor near Slocum's boots. "Have you been wearing that since you rode into town?"

"Yes."

"Don't you know there's an ordinance against carrying guns in McKalb?"

Slocum rolled his eyes and let out a measured sigh. "I told

22

a few deputies I'd go to the sheriff's office. At least, I think they were deputies."

"Were they a couple anxious boys with baby fat still on their cheeks?" she asked.

"Sounds like them."

"That's Lyle and Wes. They do most of the footwork for the sheriff. Anything happens, and they go running back to White like a couple of puppies who just caught their first rabbit. This is probably just them trying to act like important men."

Kate tapped a few more times on the door and said, "Miss Sayers. The sheriff is *downstairs*. You should—"

"Come out right now," another voice demanded. This one was gruff and overpowering compared to Kate's urgent yet meek tone.

Quickly fussing with her dress and hair to make herself more presentable, Nellie hissed, "If you've got something to keep from the law, just be quick about it and tell me."

"It's just the damn gun," Slocum growled. "I've got nothing to hide, so I'll step outside with you right now. That is, unless you'd rather not have people talking about us being in here together."

She dismissed that with an impatient wave. "I don't give a damn what anyone thinks. With all the scandal I see while running my hotels, folks around here have already said all they can say about me." After one last tug on her dress, Nellie stood up straight, put on a cordial smile, and walked toward the door. Just as she was reaching for the handle, a series of harder knocks rattled it in its frame.

"The sheriff needs a word with you, Miss Sayers," the gruff voice said.

Nellie pulled open the door to reveal the bearded deputy with his hand still poised for another knock. "Hello, Wes," she said. "There must be a real emergency to warrant all this commotion."

The deputy lowered his hand and loosened the fist he'd made. When he spotted Slocum inside the room, he moved his hand down a bit lower so it hung within a few inches of the pistol holstered at his hip. "Are you in any danger, Miss Sayers?"

"No. Why would I be in danger? You're the one knocking my door down."

"Do you know that man?"

"Yes. John's a good friend."

Although the blonde from the front desk might have snickered at that any other time, she looked too nervous to do so now.

Rather than let anyone go through more uncomfortable small talk, Slocum stepped forward until he was practically nose to nose with the young lawman. "Did you come all this way to give me some more grief?"

"Come downstairs," Wes said evenly. "The sheriff wants to have a word with you."

"Did you find your badge or should I just take it on faith you're the law around here?"

Nellie smacked Slocum's shoulder just hard enough to get his attention. "Don't give Wes any more lip," she scolded. "He's as much a deputy as you are a pain in the rump."

Slocum shrugged and said, "Sounds like she's got us both pegged. Perhaps I can save you the trouble, Wes." With that, Slocum reached for his Colt and eased it from its holster. Even though he took his sweet time clearing leather, the deputy nearly jumped out of his boots. "Take it easy, kid," Slocum growled as he held the gun so it was pointed at the floor.

The deputy kept his hand on his own weapon and looked as if he thought he might be taking his last breaths right then and there. When Slocum emptied the six-shooter's cylinder, the deputy looked even more surprised. He didn't know what to do when Slocum flipped the Colt around to offer him its handle.

"Go on," Slocum said. "I meant to see the sheriff myself, but if the law doesn't have anything else better to do around here, check my gun in and we can all get back to our business."

Keeping one hand on his own pistol, Wes reached out with his other as if he was attempting to snatch a piece of meat from a hungry dog's mouth. With one quick yet fumbling motion, he grabbed Slocum's Colt and stepped back. "Come with me."

"Aw, hell, I still need to see the sheriff?" Slocum groused. When he looked over at Nellie, all he got was a shrug.

"You wanted to give lip to the deputies," she said.

Slocum sighed and shook his head. Walking past the young lawman, he couldn't help but feel like he still might catch a bullet in the back. Once he was in the hall, Slocum stopped and let the deputy move to where Slocum could keep an eye on him. Wes motioned for Slocum to move along, but wasn't about to get close enough to add a shove. That way, Slocum was able to angle himself so he wasn't presenting his back as an open target for the fidgety lawman.

It was a quiet, nervous walk to the lobby. Before he'd made it halfway down the stairs, Slocum could see a small group gathered there waiting for him. Sheriff White was easy enough to spot. He was the only man who stood his ground and wasn't fidgeting as Wes and Slocum came into view. He was just shy of average height, but had the build of a man who'd worked for everything he ever owned. His name could very well have been an accurate description of the man, because his entire head was covered in a thick layer of neatly trimmed hair and whiskers. Not only did he have the air of authority about him, but he was the only man who wore a badge in plain sight.

Slocum put on a friendly smile and said, "Good to meet you, Sheriff. This town sure knows how to welcome a newcomer."

"You're John Slocum?" the lawman asked.

"That's right. Before you ask for my gun, I already handed it over to your deputy. And before you ask, I have indeed been told about the town's ordinance. I also told your men I was going to pay you a visit."

Sheriff White nodded slowly as he listened to Slocum, but

didn't acknowledge him any more than that. Glancing over at Wes, he asked, "He handed over his gun peacefully?"

"Yes, sir, Sheriff," Wes said as he walked forward to present the Colt Navy. As soon as the deputy moved past Slocum, his clean-shaven partner drew a pistol and aimed it at Slocum.

"Whoa there," Nellie said as she hurried downstairs. "John handed over his gun, so there's no need for all of this."

"Step back, Nell," White said. "I'm handling this."

Slocum didn't like what he saw, and Nellie seemed to be just as riled up as he was. Rather than add more fuel to the fire, he kept his hands up and let her sink her teeth in.

"What's left to handle?" Nellie fumed. "You've got his gun, so take it and go! Do you honestly need to create a spectacle in my hotel on account of one man violating a town ordinance?"

"You have any other weapons, Mr. Slocum?" White asked.

"Oh, for Christ's sake!" Nellie snapped. Turning to Slocum, she asked, "What did you do to rile these boys up so much?"

"Hell if I know," Slocum replied. When he started to lower his arms, both deputies raised their gun hands to cover him. Sheriff White wasn't as jumpy, but he placed his hands on the pistols holstered in his double rig.

"This can turn real bad for you real quick," White promised. "Whatever move you make will be real slow, or it'll be your last."

Slocum knew a lawman needed to assert himself sometimes, but this was crossing a line. He studied the face of each lawman to see if he might have wronged the man in some other place at some other time. So far, Slocum was coming up short.

"Why don't you pat down Mr. Slocum, Wes," the sheriff said. "See if he's carryin' anything else we should know about."

"What's the matter?" Slocum snarled. "Is there an ordinance against carrying pocket watches or too many cigars?"

"No," White snapped, "but I can sure write one up if you want to keep testing my patience."

When Sheriff White said those words, everyone within earshot held their tongue.

Nellie was the first to break the silence, and she did so very carefully. "Nobody's putting up a fight. John handed his gun over. I don't see what the fuss is about."

"There won't be no fuss if Mr. Slocum hands over any other weapons he might be carrying."

"There's a knife in my boot," Slocum announced.

One of the deputies stuck the barrel of his pistol in Slocum's gut as he stooped to take the knife away. Just to be certain, he also patted Slocum down from head to toe. "That's all he's got," Wes announced.

White nodded slowly and said, "All right then. Come along with us now, Mr. Slocum."

"If there's a fine to be paid, I can do it right now," Slocum said.

"You can do that in my office."

Slocum gritted his teeth and went over every step he'd taken since arriving in McKalb. He'd seen the sign and all but ignored it. He'd seen the deputies and given them a hard time because they'd seemed like twitchy little punks. Perhaps he'd overstepped his bounds a bit, so he figured he deserved to take some grief in return. Besides that, he was curious to see what the lawmen would do when he didn't give them a chance to fight. If things went to hell too quickly, Slocum had already sized up the lawmen and figured he could get through them if the need arose. He held his hands up high and allowed himself to be shoved by the deputy.

"Don't fret, Nellie," Slocum said to the hotel's owner before she got worked up all over again. "I can handle myself."

"All the same," she replied, "I'll come down to that office to make sure they treat you right." She shifted her eyes to Sheriff White and added, "One of my business partners is a lawyer. Maybe you've heard of The Terror of Sacramento. If things get pushed too far either way, I'm sure he'll have some good advice."

"I'm sure he will," White said with a tip of his hat. "You give Daniel my best."

Slocum was escorted from the hotel with a deputy on either side. The sheriff walked a few paces ahead. The skies had darkened considerably since Slocum had arrived, and the streets were fairly well lit by a series of lanterns hanging from posts along the street. It wasn't enough to illuminate every storefront, but it allowed the procession to move along without tripping in the dark.

The few locals they passed watched them while leaning against posts or peeking from windows without doing much more than giving a quick nod or a wave. Even though Slocum had been in a lot worse spots than this, he couldn't help feeling like a man being led to a freshly constructed set of gallows. Fortunately, the only thing at the end of their walk was a modest little building near the end of a narrow street.

Sheriff White's office was lit by a single candle that sputtered at the edge of a tidy desk. Upon entering, one of the deputies took the candle and walked around to light a few lanterns. Slocum was shoved into a cage built into the back corner of the office before there was enough light to see the bars.

Wes opened the door to the cell while the clean-shaven deputy said, "Empty your pockets."

Slocum had to think for a moment, but came up with a name Nellie had mentioned a little while ago. "You're Lyle, right?"

"Empty yer pockets."

He dug out a bit of money, a pocket watch, and a few other bits and pieces that didn't amount to much. Slocum piled it all onto a table near the cell and shrugged. "If you're looking for a bribe, you're shit out of luck." When he saw the grim looks on the men's faces, Slocum added, "That was just a joke, fellas."

"Get into that cell and I'll sing you a song in return," Sheriff White said.

Slocum stepped into the cage and waited for Lyle to shut and lock the door. It was pretty clear he wasn't going to get the song he'd been promised.

The cell was about the size of a broom closet. There was something against the wall that was either a small cot or a low table. The floor stank of piss and the walls creaked loudly with the slightest touch. Rather than try to put his weight on the cot, Slocum grabbed the bars in front of him and leaned on them. "How long do I have to stay in here?"

"As long as it takes," White said as he settled in behind his desk.

"Is there a fine I need to pay?"

"Not yet."

Slocum's plan had been to spend the next few hours paying for his smart mouth and have a hearty breakfast in the morning. He'd spent plenty of nights in jail after drinking more than his share of whiskey. Usually, those accommodations were better than sleeping in the stable with his horse, and were a hell of a lot cheaper than a hotel. Something about this just didn't sit well with him, however, and it had nothing to do with the stench the previous prisoners had left behind.

Forcing himself to remain as civil as possible, Slocum said, "You can't just toss me into a cage without telling me what I need to do to get out."

The sheriff sifted through some papers and scribbled something onto one of them while his deputies looked over Slocum's belongings. None of the lawmen seemed willing to respond to what had been said.

"I figure I'll be out in the morning," Slocum announced.

That got a chuckle from Wes, but not much else.

"There's a fine to be paid, right? I can get you the money." Still nothing.

"Look, I'm just trying to see what I need to do to—"

"What you can do," Sheriff White cut in, "is shut your damn mouth and get comfortable in that cell."

"And if you want yer guts splattered all over them walls," Wes added, "you just need to give me a reason to pull my trigger."

"Shut the hell up, Wes," White snapped.

On any other day, seeing Wes back down like a dog scampering to hide under the porch with its tail between its legs would have been amusing. Now, the only thing that would have brought a smile to Slocum's face was seeing that jail door swing open. Slocum shook his head, turned his back to the lawmen, and went to his cot. "You men need to keep yourself busy by railroading me into a jail cell? Fine. If this is how you assholes enforce an ordinance against carrying firearms, then I guess this town's about the safest place in the goddamn country."

"You can cut that horseshit right now," Sheriff White said. "Ain't a man in here who thinks you're in that cell on account of carrying a gun."

"Really?" Slocum grunted. "Then what's my crime?"

White looked up from his paperwork, crossed one last t, and said, "Murder. Once you're dragged out of McKalb, this town will be a whole lot safer."

4

"Murder?" Slocum asked.

Sheriff White nodded.

"And who am I supposed to have murdered?" When he didn't get an answer, Slocum rattled his cage. "Goddammit, answer me!"

Both deputies raised their weapons while Sheriff White calmly reached down to grab a shotgun that must have been propped behind his desk. Slocum was so riled up that he barely took notice of the weapons.

"I suggest you simmer down," White said. "According to the notice, it don't matter much if you're handed over in irons or in a box."

"What notice?"

White cocked his head to one side and walked around his desk. He maneuvered around the furniture, grabbed a piece of paper with one hand, and made his way to the cell, all without taking his eyes off Slocum. His deputies, on the other hand, fidgeted as if they'd cornered a rabid dog.

Stopping just outside of any prisoner's reach, White leveled his shotgun at Slocum and held up a notice with his other hand. "See for yourself."

The notice was a standard posting offering a reward for a wanted criminal that read:

> *John Slocum WANTED for the murder of Patrick Chesterton. A reward of $15,000 offered by Chesterton Mining Co. for bringing this killer to offices in town of Shackley, Dakota Territory. Genuine proof of Slocum's death also acceptable.*

"I must say," White grumbled, "catching our attention the way you did was awful sloppy."

As angry as Slocum was, he'd found a new target for it. "That's because I don't know anyone named Patrick Chesterton and I sure as hell didn't kill him. I haven't even set foot in a place called Shackley."

"If you're wanted for murder, why would you say any different?"

"Yeah!" Wes chimed in. "Especially to lawmen." After making his statement, he looked back and forth between the sheriff and the other deputy for some kind of acknowledgment. When he didn't get it, he shut his mouth and continued pointing his gun at the cage.

Slocum took a deep breath, loosened his grip on the bars, and forced himself to speak in a calmer tone. "Just because someone prints up some notices, that doesn't make it open season on a man."

"This notice is real enough," White protested.

"Then it's a lie. Aren't you even gonna look into it and see what the hell's behind this?"

White shook his head just enough for it to be seen. "I only post ones that come from good sources. I asked around about you, Mr. Slocum. From what I heard, the claims in this notice don't seem too far-fetched. You might even get a trial when you get to the Dakota Territory."

"You think whoever wrote that notice wants a trial?" Slocum asked.

After thinking it over for all of two seconds, White

shrugged and walked back to his desk. "Ain't my place to guess about things like that. You'd best get comfortable because you're headed for the Dakota Territory as soon as the man we notified comes to collect you."

That marked the end of the conversation. Both deputies knew as much and backed away from the cell. Slocum could tell he would have more luck pleading his case to a stump, so he bit his tongue. Lyle had a few words with the sheriff before leaving the office, but Wes plopped onto a stool so he could watch Slocum with his pistol lying across his knee. The sheriff scribbled on some more papers, but acted as if the cell and the man inside it no longer existed.

Slocum didn't bother trying to get any of the lawmen's attention. It was clear they'd already made up their minds and intended on following the notice to the letter. Since none of those letters seemed to care whether Slocum stayed alive or not, he sat on his cot and kept his mouth shut.

If the cage seemed small before, it seemed doubly so when Slocum tried to stretch out on a cot that was big enough to support him from his head to just short of his knees. His boots poked through the bars at that end of the cell, but the lawmen must have been used to that. Slocum stared up at the roof, folded his arms across his chest, and let a flurry of thoughts stream through his head.

Not only had he been accused of murdering a complete stranger, but whoever had done the accusing had also put a sizable reward on Slocum's head. He was no stranger to being on the wrong end of a bounty, but normally he had some inkling of why that money was being offered. If he'd come across the information some other time, Slocum might have shrugged it off and chalked it up to any one of a number of assholes out there who wanted to see him dead. Being stuck in a cell and a few hours away from someone collecting that reward, however, made the matter much more pressing.

At that moment, he couldn't help but think about what he'd been doing a scant hour ago. It seemed like years since he'd been rolling around with Nellie on silk sheets. Before that, he'd had a hell of a good meal, and before that, he'd been riding without a care in the world. All that time, some asshole had made up a lie about a murder, and put the word out for Slocum to be brought in dead or alive. In the quiet office, the grinding of his own teeth filled Slocum's ears.

Even worse was the stench filling his nostrils. All he had to do was glance over to his left to see the warped boards that other prisoners must have used for an outhouse. Since there wasn't a pot or anything else in there, Slocum guessed he'd probably have to do the same. Before he could add that to his list of things to be mad about, Slocum heard a passing breeze rattle the office walls. More importantly, he could feel some of that breeze leak in from between a few nearby slats.

Suddenly, the door to the office was pushed open and the two remaining lawmen jumped to their feet. "Where is he?" Nellie asked. Spotting the cage before the sheriff or the deputy could respond, she stomped forward and said, "This is ridiculous. I'll pay the fine right now, so just unlock that door!"

"There's no fine and there'll be no unlocking that door," White told her.

"Why? Tell me why!"

The sheriff took her by her arm and led her outside. Although Slocum didn't make a move to prevent any of that from happening, the deputy still aimed his gun at him and shot a warning glare toward the cell. Slocum sat with his back against the wall and tried burning holes through the office's front door. No sparks flew, but the door did come open after a few minutes.

Sheriff White poked his head in and said, "Step outside for a bit, Wes."

The deputy seemed confused when Nellie walked in, but shrugged and headed out the door. Nellie approached the cage and fretted for a few seconds as White shut the door and then sat down behind his desk. Finally, she whispered, "The sheriff told me about the notice."

"Yeah?"

"Is that why you came here? To hide from whoever's looking for you?"

"First of all," Slocum grunted, "I never laid eyes on the man that was killed. And second, if I truly had anything to do with that murder and wanted to hide out, I'd go a lot farther than this."

Nellie's eyes widened a bit. "So you didn't kill that man?"

"You thought I did?"

She winced, and then shrugged as if to apologize for it. After glancing back at White's desk, she whispered, "You've killed men before, John. You told me so."

"Yeah, but not this one."

"So who would post such a thing in that notice?"

"I don't know, but I need to find out. At the very least, I need to get the hell out of this cage."

Sheriff White sat behind his desk, scribbling his notes, but didn't seem overly concerned with whatever he heard. A man in his position probably heard something similar from anyone locked up in that cell.

"Should I bring my lawyer friend over here?" Nellie asked. "Perhaps he could help."

"More than likely, he'd just go along with the notice. Even if he didn't, I doubt he could get me out of here before I'm dragged into the Dakota Territory."

"You don't know that. When are you leaving?"

"Tomorrow morning," Sheriff White said.

She gritted her teeth and pulled in a hissing breath. "That soon?"

"Anyone chasing a bounty tends to move pretty quick," Slocum grunted. He stood up and leaned against the bars. When he saw Sheriff White take notice of that, Slocum muttered, "I'm really sorry about all of this. I sure didn't mean for any trouble to come your way."

Nellie stepped closer and started to touch his shoulder, but was stopped by a grunt from White. Keeping her hands folded, she cooed, "I know, John. I just wish I could get you out of there."

"Maybe you shouldn't worry about it." He dropped his voice a bit more as though he didn't want his words rattling throughout the entire office. "Sometimes, a man's just gotta face his problems the right way. Promise not to think any less of me."

Casting a glance toward the sheriff, Nellie leaned closer to Slocum and whispered, "Why would you even think that?"

This time, Slocum noticed that Sheriff White was no longer looking up from his work.

Speaking in a quick whisper that was barely loud enough for Nellie to hear, Slocum said, "You need to help me get out of here."

"I don't think I—"

"Keep your voice down and listen. I don't mean out of this cage. I mean out of this town."

She was reluctant at first, but eventually, Nellie turned her back to the sheriff and matched Slocum's barely audible tone. "What are you talking about now?"

"With that reward being offered, bounty hunters will come after me even if I do get out of here. I got enough grief without that kind of mess. I'll find my way out of this jail, but things would go a lot smoother if I had my horse nearby and waiting for me. Think you could do that?"

"I don't want to be a party to a jailbreak. I've got a business to worry about."

"Then just . . . send someone to . . . aw, to hell with it. I'll go it alone."

Sheriff White stirred behind his desk and seemed ready to come over to the cell, so Nellie nodded at Slocum and raised her voice just enough for it to be clear she wasn't trying to keep it from being heard. "Did you take part in that murder, John?"

"No," Slocum replied as he stared directly into Nellie's eyes. "I didn't."

"Tell me what you need."

Since that question wasn't necessarily sinister, Sheriff

White didn't seem to mind the fact that Slocum whispered his response.

"Get my horse ready for a long ride and tie it up somewhere close," he said.

Nellie nodded and continued her heartwarming charade for the sheriff's benefit. "Of course, darling."

"If anyone asks, you don't know about anything that happened after you leave here."

"Naturally."

"That's it."

When Nellie reached through the bars to touch Slocum's hand, the sheriff stood up and walked toward the cell. "That's long enough," he said. "You'll need to say your good-byes."

Slocum thought she was overdoing it a little when she dabbed her eyes as if she was close to tears, but the sheriff seemed to buy her act well enough. He took her gently by the elbow and escorted her toward the front door. Nellie and White talked, but Slocum didn't listen to any of that. Instead, he watched how far away from the cell White was willing to go, and was pleasantly surprised when the lawman actually stepped outside for a few moments.

This might just be easier than Slocum had hoped.

The night was quiet and uneventful. Slocum got a second dinner, which consisted of a bowl of biscuits and gravy brought to him by Wes. He picked at the biscuits, but left the gravy for later.

"Hey," Slocum grunted after his biscuits had formed a lump in his stomach. "I gotta take a piss."

"Hold it."

"Until morning?"

Wes pulled a watch from his pocket and then hopped up from his stool. "Or piss in yer hand. I don't give a shit which it is, since I'm leavin'."

"You'll leave when Lyle comes to spell you," Sheriff White said from behind the newspaper that had kept him busy once all of his work was done. When he didn't get a response from his deputy, White lowered a corner of the newspaper and glared at the younger man.

"Fine," Wes grunted. Looking at Slocum, he snapped, "And don't even think about messin' that floor! Drunks already turned that cell into a damn sty."

Even though he'd been in the cage for a while, Slocum still wasn't used to the smell. Since the first moment that stench had hit his nose, Slocum had arrived at the opinion that the soiled boards could prove to be more of a help than a hindrance. Lying on his cot, he let one arm dangle over the side until his hand brushed against the back wall. The boards were warped and mildewed from moisture and God only knows what else. Slocum pushed against a few of them, and found one or two that had some give. They weren't exactly loose, but they weren't too solid either. Even if he relieved his bladder on the rotten spot, it would still be rough to slip out through the narrow opening. Fortunately, he had a little something to aid that situation.

Huffing loudly, Slocum stood and picked up the bowl he'd been given for supper. All that remained were some biscuit crumbs and a puddle of greasy gravy. He dipped his fingers into the gravy, stuck them in his mouth, and immediately spat grease out. "This is some putrid slop!" he said, "Don't I at least get some real food?"

"It was good enough for us, so it'll be good enough for you," White commented.

"It ain't good enough for a damned pig." With that, Slocum kicked his cot and pitched his bowl into the back corner. Although he hadn't broken the bowl as he'd intended, his aim was good enough to splatter the grease onto the warped boards. Unfortunately, his cot was nailed to the floor and wouldn't come away from the wall.

"Hey!" Wes barked. "Calm down in there!"

Before Slocum came up with some more hell to raise, he was provided with an even better distraction. The office's door was opened by the second deputy, who entered and took in the scene. "Looks like I'm just in time," Lyle said.

"I knew you two couldn't watch a single prisoner without my help."

Wes stomped toward the door, waving at the cell as if he was trying to clear out a cloud of dirty smoke. "You can sure as hell do it without me. I'm gettin' a drink and some sleep."

"How about a drink for me?" Slocum asked.

"Piss into yer bowl and drink that," the deputy said on his way out.

"What?" Slocum snarled. "Say that to my face! You wanna know why you won't do that? Because you know you'll get this!" He spun around and kicked his cot. When it didn't come loose, he kicked it even harder while adding, "And *this*!"

Sheriff White took a few steps toward the cell, placed his hand on one of his holstered guns, and told Slocum, "You'll get some of this if you don't rein it in right about now."

Slocum had felt the cot break loose from its moorings, so he did as he was told. Some of the other times when he'd been locked up for whatever reason, Slocum had seen prisoners pitching fits somewhat similar to the one he'd just thrown. Back then, he'd always wanted to be the one to shut those assholes up. But there was a method to his madness. The nails holding the cot's front two legs to the floor had been pried up, and the other two nails looked to have been loosened considerably.

"Has he been like this all night?" Lyle asked. "No wonder Wes was so anxious to get out of here."

"He's been grousing, but he ain't been this ornery," White replied. "If he tries to interrupt us again, we'll just have to make sure his trip tomorrow is made even more uncomfortable than that cot." Since Slocum didn't dig himself into a deeper hole, the sheriff nodded and waved the deputy over. "Take a look at this here map. I'm plotting our man's ride into Shackley."

"Why don't one of us just take him?" the deputy grunted.

"You ever hauled a dangerous man across so many miles?"

"No, but I can drag a dead carcass into the Dakota Territory."

"Save the tough talk," White declared. "The man I contacted is someone I can trust. He'll get the job done right, get the most money he can get, and bring us our rightful share. Also, he'll be able to know if this is the John Slocum we're after or not. Since there ain't no picture on this notice, I won't hand over any man to any bounty hunter unless I know I'm handing over the right man. That's that. Now come over here and help me with this."

The shadows in Slocum's cell were more than thick enough to hide the smirk that crawled onto his face. When neither lawman was looking in his direction, he gripped the sides of his cot and slowly pried the other two legs free from the floor. The nails creaked within the wood a bit, but didn't make a lot of noise thanks to the grease that had been spilled. Once the cot was loose, Slocum was able to scoot it away from the wall. The office wasn't very well lit and the cell was in the darkest corner, but he didn't want to push his luck by being too obvious. Rather than move the cot too much, he scooted it just far enough away from the wall to give him some room to work.

The two lawmen were busy, so Slocum lay on his side on the cot and reached out with both hands to press against the lower boards. He did his best to keep from thinking about just how many coatings of piss had been required to rot away that wood. The spilled gravy covered up some of the stench, but that bit of help ended once Slocum cracked a board to expose the rotted inner layers. When that smell hit him, he nearly gagged.

"Hey over there," the sheriff said.

Slocum's stomach clenched. The notion of being caught so early forced him to think of how many different ways he could fight his way out of that office. Of course, that might only serve to put an even bigger price on his head.

Sheriff White asked, "You still need to use the privy?"

Relieved in more ways than one, Slocum replied, "Yeah, I

do." As he rolled onto his other side, something was tossed at him that rattled against the bars and landed half inside the cell.

"Put those on then."

The things that had been tossed at him were handcuffs, and Slocum fitted the clunky iron rings around one wrist and shut it. The other wrist was a little tougher, but he managed to wrap that one in iron as well. As Sheriff White approached the cell, Slocum stood close to the bars with his hands held out for inspection.

"Stand back," White said.

Slocum backed up, but his legs almost immediately hit the cot. Rather than make noise by pushing the cot back into place, Slocum shuffled his feet a few more times to make it sound as though he'd backed up the appropriate distance. Either White didn't notice the cot or wasn't paying such close attention, because he unlocked the cell door and stepped back.

"Come on out," White said as he smoothly drew one of his Smith & Wesson pistols. "And don't get any ideas."

Too late for that. Slocum had plenty of ideas.

5

Slocum's trip to the outhouse was a genuine event. He and White shuffled from the office like a funeral procession while Lyle stayed behind to watch from the office's front door. Both lawmen had their guns drawn and pointed at Slocum at all times. When he was doing his business in the outhouse, Slocum had no doubt those guns were still pointed in his direction.

The trip wasn't a complete waste of time, however. First of all, Slocum did need to use the privy. Second, he'd spotted his gun belt hanging from a peg behind Sheriff White's desk. Third, he spotted his horse tied to a post no more than twenty yards from the outhouse. He didn't expect Nellie to be so quick to fulfill her task, but it did him some good to see the gray stallion saddled up and ready to go. Hopefully, there weren't any horse thieves bold enough to try their luck so close to the sheriff's office.

Slocum was led back to his cell and locked up without incident. Once again, both lawmen were more concerned with watching him than paying attention to what had been moved inside the cage itself. After he was locked up, the cuffs were taken off and both men went back to their posts. Slocum gave them another hour or two to get settled before starting in on some work of his own.

His task wasn't very complicated, but it took some effort. Because of the poor condition of the wall, the hardest part was to keep from making any noise while prying the lowest boards loose. If he'd been so inclined, he could have shoved the cot aside and kicked the damn wall apart. Of course, he also would have been shot full of holes before he could get outside. Not wanting to tempt his good fortune at having been locked into a shoddy jail cell meant for tired drunks, Slocum lay on his side, stretched out his arm, and kept pushing against the soggy, mildewed boards.

Sometime past midnight, the weakest of those boards gave way. The wood was so soaked through that it made more of a soft crunching sound than the crack of breaking lumber. The gust of fresh air that came soon after was more than welcome after he'd spent so long with his face next to all that squalor. Slocum rolled onto his other side so he could get a look at the two lawmen watching over him.

Sheriff White sat with his feet propped on his desk, a book in his hands, and his head angled down. Slocum put the odds at fifty-fifty as to whether the sheriff was reading or asleep. Lyle shifted on his stool, flipping through one of the sheriff's newspapers. Slocum only had to wait for another hour or so before one of the men got restless.

"Be right back," Lyle grunted as he stood up and stretched his legs. "Just need to skip to my lou."

"Nature calls," White replied.

Apparently, the sheriff's interpretation of the deputy's comment was accurate, because Lyle left the office and headed straight for the outhouse. Slocum could see as much through the hole he'd made in his wall, and decided this was the time to make his move. Waiting any longer would only mean someone with fresher eyes would be watching him.

As soon as the sheriff dipped his head again, Slocum eased himself off the side of the cot closest to the wall. He lowered himself onto the floor and scooted toward the hole before realizing another potential problem: The hole he'd made had looked a lot bigger than it actually was.

Slocum eased one arm out through the space where the slat had been, followed by his shoulder. Twisting his head to one side was enough to get that through, but only after scraping the hell out of one ear. All this time, he'd done his best to keep from making noise, hoping that the shadows in his cell were thick enough to cover his escape. There was the possibility that Sheriff White had already spotted him, but it was too late for Slocum to worry about that now. If he stopped, he'd just be wedged half in and half out. If he kept going, he at least had a chance at getting all the way out.

In the end, Slocum's long ride to McKalb wound up as the determining factor. Rather than spend too much time eating home-cooked meals or town food, he'd been making due with jerked beef, oatmeal, and beans. When he'd gotten sick of that, he'd taken to eating like a bird that occasionally pecked at some reliable staples. That diet had whittled his body down to something lean enough to squeeze through a hole in the wall without getting stuck for more than a few seconds here or there. The piss-soaked wood and the grease that had been spilled earlier allowed him to squirm all the way outside without making enough noise to draw the sheriff's attention.

He hadn't even been locked up for an entire day, but Slocum felt overjoyed to get the hell out of that cell. His horse was in sight, but his gun was hanging on the wall behind the sheriff. In the few seconds it took for him to think about that, he heard a grunt from the outhouse, followed by the rattle of a latch on the privy's door. Lyle pulled it open and stepped outside before Slocum could find a place to hide.

"What in the hell?" Lyle grunted.

Before the deputy could say or do anything else, Slocum lowered his shoulder and rushed him like a bull. There wasn't a lot of ground to cover between the office and the outhouse, but Slocum felt like he'd been running a mile before he slammed into Lyle's gut. The deputy had been getting ready to shout for help and the impact drove all the air from his lungs.

Lyle was almost knocked off his feet, and barely managed to keep his legs under him as he was shoved toward the outhouse. His back hit the crooked doorway, but his momentum carried him partly inside before he reached out to grab whatever he could. Hanging on to the edge of the doorway, Lyle regained his composure and brought his knee straight up into Slocum's chest.

It was a solid hit, but Slocum barely felt it land. As soon as he saw Lyle reach for the gun at his hip, Slocum pulled the deputy closer and drove his other fist into Lyle's face. The crack of knuckles against jaw broke through the late-night calm like a shot from a cannon. Slocum followed that one with another, but Lyle twisted around to absorb the second punch on the side of his head.

Lyle blinked a few times in surprise and snapped his head forward to butt against Slocum's face. About an inch and a half to the right and it would have caught the bridge of Slocum's nose. The deputy wasn't the only one who had the sand to take some punishment, and Slocum took his lumps well enough to keep fighting.

Since slamming the deputy against the outhouse would have only created more noise, Slocum grabbed the younger man's shirt in both hands and hauled him into the open. As Lyle was trying to get his bearings after being swung about, Slocum stampeded straight into him with an outstretched arm that caught the deputy squarely between the neck and shoulders. Lyle practically folded around Slocum's arm before dropping heavily to the ground. To his credit, he managed to pull his pistol from its holster before Slocum could stop him. Even so, Lyle wasn't fast enough to fire a shot before Slocum's boot pinned his gun hand against the dirt.

Lyle didn't release the gun right away and Slocum hoped the hammer wasn't about to drop. Whether it hit him or not, any shot would be loud enough to draw the sheriff and probably several other locals out to investigate. Slocum leaned down on the foot he'd used to trap the deputy's arm until he felt Lyle's hand crunch under the weight. "You gonna let go of that gun or should I ground your hand into dust?" he asked.

The deputy tried to speak, but could only grunt in pain.

Slocum bent down and snatched the gun away from the deputy. Pointing the six-shooter down at its owner, Slocum said, "Get up and don't make a sound."

"You're gonna make plenty of noise when you pull that trigger. After that, the sheriff will come out here and blast you in half."

"If I'd wanted you dead, I would have shot you up close without making much noise at all. Or," Slocum added, "I could have snapped your neck while you were still in the shitter."

Seeing the resignation in the deputy's eyes, Slocum stepped back and waggled the gun. "Get up."

The young lawman did as he was told. Although he didn't purposely make a lot of noise, the scraping of his boots seemed to echo throughout the sleeping town.

"Unbuckle your pants and get into the outhouse."

Although still nervous at being at gunpoint, Lyle scowled and asked, "What did you say?"

"You heard me," Slocum said.

The deputy unbuckled his belt and shuffled into the out-house.

"Now make your belt into a loop and stick your arms and legs through it."

"I . . . don't think it's big enough for that."

"Sure it is," Slocum said as he glanced toward the office. "You'll either do it yourself or I'll crack you upside the head with this pistol and do it for you."

Grudgingly, the deputy pulled his belt from its loops and then threaded one end through the buckle. He sat on the bench in the outhouse, lowered his feet through the belt, and then did the same with his hands. It was awkward, but he

managed to hold the belt in place by stretching his arms out
to keep it from falling.

"Good job," Slocum said. He then stepped forward and
said, "Now open your mouth."

Lyle lost more color in his face than when he'd first found
himself at the wrong end of his own gun. "Oh, Lord."

"Nothing like that, dumb shit," Slocum growled as he
stuck the gun barrel into the deputy's mouth. "I wasn't
locked up long enough for you to turn my head."

Having the gun barrel in such a precarious spot made the
deputy sit real still when Slocum reached down to grab
the belt and cinch it tight around Lyle's arms and legs. The
leather was worn enough for him to get it buckled using
only one hand and a bit of leverage. Once that was done,
Slocum followed up on another promise by cracking Lyle
upside the head with the pistol. The deputy slumped over
into a very uncomfortable bundle on the floor of the outhouse. Slocum closed the door and dropped the latch in
place. The latch could be opened from either side of the
door, but Lyle wouldn't exactly have an easy time of it
whenever he woke up. Besides that, Slocum didn't intend
on being anywhere close when that happened. He did, however, have one more matter to attend to before leaving.

Slocum already had a gun. It just wasn't his gun. While
that wasn't particularly crucial, it might be easily fixed.
Lyle wasn't making a peep, and nobody had stormed out of
the office, so Slocum guessed his escape was going pretty
well. Perhaps he was feeling lucky when he snuck back
toward the office to reclaim his own gun belt and pistol. At
least, he had enough sense to keep sneaking past the door
to get a look through one of the side windows closest to
White's desk.

Standing to the side of that window, Slocum inched over
until he could barely get a look through the glass. The angle
was just good enough to see part of the sheriff's face. White
was sleeping, all right. Either that, or he liked to read with
his eyes drooped shut and his head lolling forward. Slocum

moved to the front door, hoping he hadn't made one hell of a mistake in not cutting his losses several minutes ago.

The door opened easily and without a squeak. Slocum stayed in the shadows for a few seconds. If White was still awake, Slocum could always wait for the man to come out to check on his deputy and then bushwhack him. It seemed there was no need for anything so drastic, so Slocum pushed the front door open and took a step inside.

White didn't move.

Slocum made a quick pass around the sheriff's desk, snagged his gun belt, and moved along. His gun still hung in the leather holster, providing no more reason for Slocum to remain in that office. Without so much as a sideways glance toward the cage in the far corner, Slocum moved outside and eased the door shut behind him.

Buckling his gun belt around his waist, Slocum had the urge to let out a joyous yelp. After he'd been cooped up in that filthy cell on account of a lie that would probably lead to his neck getting stretched, breaking out of there was almost better than the time he'd spent with Nellie. Almost, but not quite.

He resisted the urge to go see her one last time to show his appreciation as he climbed onto his horse and took up the reins.

"Hey! What are you doing?"

The question came from one of the houses closest to the sheriff's office. It was just as dark as all the other nearby houses, but the door was open and a man stood on its porch. It wasn't just any man either, but the sheriff's other deputy. Apparently, Wes didn't mind living within a stone's throw of his work.

"Holy shit!" Wes grunted as he raced to the edge of his porch. "It *is* you! Don't move another muscle!"

Slocum moved every muscle required to lean down over his horse's neck and tap his heels against its sides. After that, the horse moved a few muscles as well and got them both moving toward the street.

Wes shouted and fired at Slocum, creating more than enough ruckus to wake up Sheriff White along with half the town. More shots were fired, but Slocum didn't bother drawing his pistol in response. If he'd intended on killing lawmen, he would have done it already and been gone a lot sooner. The last thing he needed was a few fresh murder charges heaped on top of the shit that had already been smeared across that reward notice. Despite all of those thoughts, Slocum's hand still went instinctively to his gun. It took a whole lot of restraint to keep from clearing leather.

The lawmen shouted at each other and fired at Slocum's back as he rode toward the edge of town. Slocum snapped his reins after turning a corner, and then snapped them again when he spotted the trail that led out of McKalb. As he was finally getting away from that town, the sound of hooves pounding against the road rumbled behind him. Slocum charged into the dark with the local law hot on his heels.

The country that had been such a beautiful sight on his way into town quickly became the bane of his existence. The hills and rocks were pretty enough in daylight, but were downright treacherous at night. He might have been in better shape if he knew the trail like the back of his hand, but that simply wasn't the case. Slocum could see about ten yards in front of him once his eyes adjusted to the shadows. When the clouds drifted away from the moon, he could tack on an extra ten yards or so to that, which wasn't much comfort when trying to hang on to a galloping horse while reloading a pistol.

For a while, Slocum thought he'd leave the steering to the animal beneath his saddle. After all, no horse wanted to trip and break its neck. That logic held up right until Slocum was forced to pull the reins to one side to avoid skidding over the top of a partially hidden boulder. Once that crisis was averted, he came up with another plan.

The lawmen were closing in on him. Slocum dismounted and led his horse off the trail. Although he was able to duck behind the boulder that had almost been the death of him,

Slocum wasn't able to get his horse out of sight before the hastily formed posse thundered around the bend.

"There he is!" Wes shouted.

Sheriff White was right behind the deputy and shouted, "Ease up now. Maybe he fell off his horse."

Once the lawmen got to about fifteen yards away from him, Slocum stepped out from behind the boulder with his gun drawn. He fired high and to the side, just to see how badly the other men could be spooked. Although his shots hissed well off target, he got the answers he'd been after. The sheriff ducked down and reined his horse to a stop, while Wes swung away from the gunfire and damn near hopped from his saddle. In his haste to get away, the deputy got one foot snagged in a stirrup and hit the ground in a heap.

Sheriff White wasn't testing anyone's mettle and he wasn't trying to get away. Instead, he raised a rifle to his shoulder with every intention of using it to put Slocum down. Slocum rushed forward to grab the rifle high up along the barrel and tried to pull it away from the lawman. White's grip remained locked, but Slocum's arm was a bit stronger. As he was yanked from his saddle, the sheriff pulled his trigger.

Slocum cursed as the rifle exploded less than a foot away from him. Even though the barrel was dangerously close, it was pointed well away from his head and sent its round into the surrounding trees. The barrel became hot as hell within Slocum's grasp and a godawful ringing filled his ears. If he hadn't been around so much gunfire for so many years, Slocum might have lost a good portion of his hearing right then and there. As it was, the only thing he lost was his grip on the rifle.

Before White could correct his position in his saddle, Slocum grabbed him by the shoulder and dragged him down. White toppled toward the ground, but Slocum hung on to keep the older man from hitting too hard. The sheriff was a tough old bird, however, and wasted no time in bringing his rifle around to fire again. Slocum kicked the rifle away a split second before it sent another bullet screaming past him. When Slocum's horse whinnied loudly, he hoped the stallion hadn't caught one of those rounds.

The older man shook free of Slocum's grip and immediately reached for one of the two pistols strapped around his waist. Although it would have been easier to knock the sheriff out, Slocum reached down to snatch the pistol from White's holster before the sheriff could get to it. His hand was still smarting from the burn he'd received, but Slocum managed to get the sheriff's weapon and aim it at him.

"Don't be foolish," Slocum warned. When he saw Wes trying to sneak around to take a shot at him, he aimed his own pistol at the deputy and added, "That goes for you, too."

"You're outnumbered!" Wes said defiantly.

Slocum backed up a step and shrugged. "Seems to me like I remedied that situation just fine. Now toss your guns away before I take more drastic steps."

"To hell with that!"

"Dammit, Wes!" Sheriff White snapped as he gingerly removed his second pistol from its holster using only a thumb and forefinger. "Don't be an idiot!"

When the deputy tossed his weapon, he did it amid a stream of obscenities that were obviously to show just how tough he truly was despite the circumstances. The show didn't have an effect on either of the other two men.

Once both lawmen were disarmed, Slocum asked, "You got more of those handcuffs?"

"Yeah," Wes replied.

"Get 'em." After the deputy had taken the cuffs from his saddlebag, Slocum said, "And the ones from the sheriff's horse. I know they're in there."

The deputy fished out a larger set that looked more like shackles intended for a man's ankles.

"Those'll do just fine," Slocum mused. "Now come over here to sit with the rest of us."

"You don't wanna make this any worse, son," Sheriff White said. "You obviously know how much trouble it is to harm a lawman. Otherwise, you wouldn't have been so careful thus far."

"Careful?" Wes spat.

Ignoring the deputy, Slocum replied, "I'd rather not kill you men, but you shouldn't force my hand. I broke out of jail, so I don't have a whole lot more to lose."

That put the fear into Wes, but didn't make much of a dent in Sheriff White.

"You got plenty to lose, son."

Slocum cocked his head. "I'm not your son, Sheriff. Wes, have a seat and clamp one of them shackles onto your ankle and the other onto his."

"This can't end well for you, Mr. Slocum," White said carefully. "You can run, but there'll be more people out looking for you. When the price on your head goes up, there'll be even more."

"I know that, which is why I intend on going somewhere nobody will find me."

"Everyone gets found," White promised. "I been a lawman long enough to know that much. You don't strike me as a bad sort, so take care of this the proper way."

Slocum had every intention of doing just that, but he didn't see any reason to share that with the two lawmen. In fact, the more convinced they were that he was going to run away from the bounty, the better. "Too late for that," he said as he straightened his arms to make sure both men could see the guns being pointed at them. "Do what I told you, Wes. Be quick about it."

The deputy looked over at the sheriff and got a reluctant nod. Only then did Wes clamp the shackles around his and White's ankles.

"Now the cuffs," Slocum said. "Same as the shackles, but on your wrists. One for him and one for you."

"I get it," Wes grunted. He carried out those orders a lot quicker than the first ones. When he was through, he and the sheriff were connected high and low by the iron restraints.

Slocum nodded approvingly at the sight before him.

While he wasn't inclined to condemn any man just for doing his job, the picture of the two law dogs wrapped up like a Christmas present brought a smile to his face. "Guess that only leaves one more thing."

As Slocum stepped back, Wes started to panic. He must have assumed the worst because he damn near squirmed out of his own skin. "More folks from town will come after us! You can't get away with killing us!"

"Be quiet," White grunted.

"I won't! *Help! Someone help!*"

The sheriff sighed and turned his head, as if he didn't want to admit knowing his deputy. "Fer Christ's sake," he muttered.

Shaking his head, Slocum holstered one pistol and used his free hand to root through the sheriff's saddlebags. He helped himself to a few supplies, but didn't take anything that amounted to more than five or six dollars. After that, he swatted the horse on the rump and let it run toward McKalb. He did the same for Wes's horse, and then added the supplies to the ones already in his own bags.

"Even if nobody comes looking, you should be able to walk back to town on your own." Climbing into his saddle, Slocum added, "If you've ever won a three-legged race, you'll do even better. Nice meetin' you gentlemen." With that, Slocum tipped his hat and rode away.

6

From head to toe, Slocum was glad to be out of that cell. His arms and legs ached from being cooped up in the cage, but felt better within minutes after going through the motions of getting away from town. There was a crimp in his back from lying on that cot, which disappeared after riding for an hour or so. Most importantly, the fresh air blowing in his face did a hell of a good job of cleaning the putrid stench from his nose.

He rode a little faster than he would have liked at first, but slowed to a more sensible pace after putting some distance between himself and the shackled lawmen. Even though he knew there would be hell to pay for breaking out of that cell and putting those three in their place, Slocum would rather answer for that than take his chances with the way things had been heading before. Sheriff White seemed like a decent fellow. Unfortunately, Slocum had seen too many lawmen turn out to be snakes with badges to put his life in the hands of someone he barely knew.

If White was the sort of man Slocum pegged him as, then he would listen to reason once the truth came out.

If McKalb's sheriff was just another in a long list of

snakes, Slocum didn't give a rat's ass what the man thought.

He headed north for a ways until he found a bed of rocks that pointed him back in the direction he truly wanted to go. After ambling along the rocks for a little while, he made his way to a stream that he'd used to fill his canteen on the way into town the day before. Rather than stop to slake his thirst, Slocum let his horse plod through the shallow water long enough to put a serious break in the tracks he'd left behind. When he found a spot on the shore that was more gravel than dirt, he steered back onto dry land and continued from there. It wasn't much longer before he found a good spot to stop and catch his breath.

Even though it felt great to be a free man again, Slocum was tired from the escape. He hadn't exactly pushed himself past his limit, but all the excitement, running, waiting, plotting, planning, and fussing had taken its toll. From the moment the lawmen had taken him into custody, Slocum had been dedicated to getting out. Now, all of that exertion came rushing back like a set of lead weights that had been dropped onto his shoulders.

Unbuckling his saddlebags, Slocum gave his horse a few friendly pats. "Glad you weren't frightened by a little gunfire, boy. Hope you're ready for another long ride."

Truth be told, the horse seemed more ready than Slocum. Its eyes were wide open and its chest swelled with every powerful breath. The stallion even switched from one foot to another as though it was anxious to get some more wind blowing through its mane.

"You'll have to cool your heels for a bit," Slocum said to the eager horse. "Let's get a look at what Nellie sent along with you."

As he said that, Slocum rummaged through the saddlebags to find a small bundle wrapped up in a bandanna and tied up with a red ribbon. He took the bundle, and couldn't help noticing several other things stuffed beneath it. Apart from the supplies he'd had in there originally, there were strips of what smelled like jerked venison, a pouch of coffee, some sandwiches, and something else that was the best sight Slocum's sore eyes could have hoped for.

"Come to Poppa," Slocum said as he grabbed hold of the bottle of whiskey. It wasn't completely full, but it was close enough. He pulled out the stopper, smelled the bottle's contents, and then took a long, greedy pull. The firewater burned a trail all the way through his body before settling into a warm little spot at the pit of his stomach. Slocum followed that with a smaller sip, which he let trickle down his throat so he could savor every last drop. By the time he let out his breath, he felt like a new man.

When he set the bottle down and tugged the ribbon to open the bundle, Slocum thought he might have drunk a bit too much of that whiskey. Shaking his head and taking another look, he realized his eyes weren't playing tricks on him. The bandanna had been wrapped around a letter and a thick stack of money.

"Good Lord," Slocum gasped.

After flipping through the bills, Slocum wrapped them up again and stuck them into the saddlebag for safekeeping. He then unfolded the letter, which had obviously been scribbled in a rush. It read:

> John,
>
> I just talked to you at the jail, so I know there's not much time. If you're reading this, then you got to your horse and are hopefully away from McKalb. Although I'd like to see you again, I don't want you anywhere near this trouble. I'll look into whatever misunderstanding brought you to that cell, but I know you can't be guilty of cold-blooded murder. Just promise me you won't do anything to make this situation worse.

"Too late for that," Slocum grunted. His stomach let out a few noises, so he dug around for some of the jerky he'd found in his bag. It was venison, all right. Damn tasty, too. While gnawing on some of that, he continued reading the letter.

> *There isn't much by way of supplies in here, but I gave you whatever I could find that might help. As for the money, it's what I intended on giving you all along. It's most of your share of the profit of my hotels. I can never thank you enough for helping me in my ventures. You're not my only partner, but you're the only one I can truly trust. The rest aren't dishonest. They're just businessmen. I used the rest of your money to pay for your horse and to keep the man at the stables from mentioning it was there at all. That comes out of your share, because you're the fool who decided to run. Come back to me in one piece.*
>
> *Yours,*
> *Nellie*

Slocum chuckled at her letter, especially the tone of the last few sentences. When he thought about some of the things she'd done with that tongue of hers, Slocum regretted leaving McKalb so soon. Rather than torture himself with thoughts like that, he spread out his bedroll and stretched out on the ground. He would be too busy watching and listening for a posse to get much sleep, but at least he could rest for a few hours until dawn.

If a posse had been formed to come after Slocum, it didn't get anywhere close to finding him. More than likely, the two lawmen had skulked back into town, hunted down a spare set of keys for their shackles, and prayed nobody had spotted them in the midst of their humiliation. There was also a chance that Sheriff White was on his way to a bigger town or contacting a more prominent lawman to search for Slocum in earnest. At the very least, he knew the sheriff's man would be sent after him once he reached McKalb. But Slocum couldn't bother himself with that. He had important work to do.

This wasn't the first time Slocum's name or likeness had wound up on a reward notice. Every so often, he'd cross paths with a bounty hunter sent by someone or other, looking for money being put up by someone else. Men like that had become annoyances in the rough road of Slocum's life. The problem with this situation was that it was spurred on by a reward that was fat enough to garner plenty of long-lasting interest. The same kind of mess had almost stretched his neck once already, and if Slocum had learned anything over the last decade or two, it was that things like this rarely dried up and blew away on their own. They either festered or got a whole lot worse. As it stood, Slocum couldn't afford either.

Also, he couldn't just sit back and let someone get away with sending a false murder charge in his direction. There was a price to pay for lies that big, and Slocum was the one to collect it.

He caught himself stewing about all of this for the better part of the next day. As he rode, he gripped his reins and glared at the eastern sky while whipping himself into a thicker lather. Finally, he had to shove those things from his head and think about something else. He was doing what needed to be done, and dwelling on it wasn't going to make the miles go by any faster.

As if to alleviate that very situation, a town came into Slocum's view. It looked to be a few miles off the trail, so he decided to stop there to stretch his legs. Besides, if Sheriff White had heard of the bounty put on his head, perhaps someone at this other town knew something as well.

That caused Slocum to reconsider.

He'd put some distance between himself and McKalb, but maybe it wasn't enough. Apart from the bounty, there was the fact that he'd put those lawmen onto their asses after breaking out of that town's sorry excuse for a jail. Perhaps it would be more prudent to stay away from other folks for a little while longer.

Slocum snapped his reins and growled, "The hell I will. Just because some asshole decides to spread lies about me don't mean I gotta abide by them."

If Slocum had wanted to sit back and hope things worked out for the best, he'd still be trying to get some sleep in Sheriff White's cage. He intended on clearing up this matter the best way he knew how. Of course, that way might get a little messy.

Slocum's first instinct was to head for the first saloon he could find. While that would have been a good place to cross paths with a bounty hunter, it would also be a good spot to run into anyone who might be looking for the fellow that busted out of the McKalb jail. Wanting to get a feel for how much dust he'd kicked up without pushing his luck any further, Slocum picked out a nice little restaurant with a good view of the main street. That way, he could get something hot in his belly while watching for any large groups of armed men who might be a posse storming through town.

The restaurant was fairly crowded. The eggs were a bit too runny and the toast was burnt, but the coffee was decent enough. Slocum didn't spot any lawmen or any groups that were big enough to be a posse. When he paid for his food, he decided to dip his toe into the waters with a few simple questions.

"Have you heard about any trouble from a town west of here?" he asked the pretty woman who settled his bill.

She had the look of a schoolteacher, but not in a matronly sort of way. Her curly hair bounced as she glanced around as if to find the answer to his question written somewhere. Finally, she admitted, "Not as such. Why?"

"I heard there might have been a shooting the other night."

"That could be anything. Maybe it was someone's birthday," she offered with a grin.

"No trouble with the law?"

"Not around here."

Slocum nodded, tipped his hat, and left. Restaurant owners and waitresses weren't exactly the source of all knowledge regarding manhunts, but they knew well enough when there was trouble brewing. Any business that catered to folks passing through town got its fair share of gossip. Emboldened by the calmness of the town, Slocum went to one of the nearby saloons. The place wasn't too busy, considering the early hour, but there were a few dedicated drinkers sitting well away from the sunlight that poured through the open door. Closing the door before any of those drunks became too cross, Slocum walked up and stood at the front corner of the bar.

"Lookin' for a room?" the barkeep asked.

Slocum would have preferred to sleep in his old cell instead of any bed provided by the filthy saloon, but declined to mention that to the man who'd offered. "No, thanks. I'll take some coffee, though."

"Same price as beer. Sure you don't wanna reconsider?"

"Coffee's fine. I'm headed into McKalb. Is that far from here?"

If the barkeep knew any news regarding McKalb, he hid it well. "Couple days maybe," the man replied while pouring a coffee-like sludge into a dented tin cup. "Follow the trail west out of town and you can't miss it."

"Any excitement over there?"

"I hear they got a fine new hotel, but the prices ain't too great. You lookin' for women, I got a few right here that'll curl your toes just fine."

"I'll bet." Slocum took one sip of his coffee, regretted it, slapped some money onto the bar, and walked out. He doubted the bartender even turned around after hearing his payment drop.

It might have been terrible coffee, but it had come along with no news. In this case, no news was most definitely good news. Rather than sit around and wait for someone to ride in and squawk about a jailbreak, Slocum mounted up and calmly left town. Since few of the locals even bothered to return his friendly glances, Slocum was confident that his presence there would be forgotten in a matter of minutes.

Before long, the trail opened up and Slocum was treated to more of the scenery that he'd enjoyed on his way into McKalb. A few banks of clouds drifted lazily across the sky to project a parade of shadows onto the ground ahead of him. Slocum alternated between letting his horse run at whatever pace it wanted and snapping the reins and putting the stallion through its paces. Either way, the horse seemed more than happy to oblige.

Sometime past noon, Slocum flipped through the money Nellie had given him. She'd either robbed a bank, or was doing even better with her hotels than Slocum had guessed. There was enough to make the trip worthwhile, despite the short stint in jail. Also, the jerked venison was spiced with just the right amount of peppers to give it a proper kick. With so much cash in his saddlebags and so much pretty country to look at, it was tough for Slocum not to savor the little things. He never forgot about the reason he was headed east, however. Although his head might have cooled off about all of the business with the reward notice, he still had his sights set squarely on his goal.

He passed through a large camp by the time the sun was dipping into the lower western sky. He didn't mention anything about McKalb, and wasn't arrested or shot on sight, so he figured it was safe to have some dinner. Before moving along, he asked the plump old lady who'd served him his pork chops a few simple questions.

"Ever hear of a place called Shackley?"

The lady crinkled her nose and fired back a question of her own. "You're intending on riding that far tonight? You can get a room here and wait until morning," she offered with a thick Italian accent. "It's not safe to ride in the dark, you know."

"I know," Slocum said. "I'll find someplace to bed down."

"That's good." When she saw the expectant look on Slocum's face, she nodded and waved her hands in a flustered tizzy. "Shackley! Oh, yes. I've heard of this place. I believe it's in the Dakotas."

"Do you know about how far it is?"

"A few days' ride, I think. We get stagecoach drivers in here all the time. They talk about stopping in at Shackley to pick up supplies and mail. Drop off, too, I think."

Sensing that was about as good as he could get from her, Slocum smiled and said, "Thanks a lot, ma'am."

After a few more kind words from the old lady, Slocum was allowed to leave. The conversation wasn't a complete waste, since a town along a stagecoach and mail route had to be a pretty good size. At the very least, it was bigger than the camp. He was about to climb into his saddle when he noticed the Italian woman watching him from her window. She waved merrily when she saw him look at her, but didn't stop staring at him. The second time he glanced over his shoulder, he found the restaurant's curtains falling back into place. Slocum led his horse around the corner before mounting it and steering for the eastern edge of camp.

Like many similar settlements, there were several cabins, wagons, and campfires around the outer perimeter of the main camp. It was dark by the time Slocum found a suitable place to spread out his bedroll and catch a few winks of sleep. Not only did he keep the bundle of money under his head like a lumpy pillow, but he kept his pistol lying across his belly where it was hidden by the rough blanket that draped over him from chest to toe. It wasn't the most comfortable sleeping arrangement, but it suited him just fine.

7

While Slocum might have started at a somewhat leisurely pace, he broke that mold once he made it into the Dakota Territory. Whenever he had a patch of level ground in front of him, he tore across it as quickly as his horse could go. He rode every night until the shadows became dangerously thick, and started again the next morning as soon as the sun gave him enough light to see.

Slocum no longer stopped at towns to see if there was news about his escape from McKalb. All he cared about was cleaning up the mess that had brought him there, and moving on. It turned out that the old Italian woman had given him a valuable tidbit of information. Shackley was easy enough to find due to the stage lines heading in and out of there. It was a well-known stop for the main routes, all of which served as beacons pointing him toward his destination. By his reckoning, he figured he'd be walking through the middle of Shackley before noon the next day. When he found out who'd printed that reward notice, Slocum wouldn't waste any time in making them regret that decision.

Something away from the trail caught Slocum's eye. A waterwheel that had been cobbled together from two wagon wheels creaked loudly enough to be heard over the pounding of his horse's hooves, and was built along the side of a river that crept like a snake along the gravel-covered terrain. A few tents hung from lines tied to two large trees, and a cooking fire sent a trail of smoke into the air. Since the ground sloped steadily downward from there, it was a good spot to get a look at the distant town. Also, the sparkling water made the river an even better spot to fill a canteen.

Slocum rode to the waterwheel and dismounted. Knowing that some folks tended to be a little skittish where their camps were concerned, he kept his hands in sight and his steps loud enough to announce his presence. Sure enough, it didn't take long for a stubby man with wide shoulders to crawl out of a little tent with a shotgun gripped in both hands.

"That's plenty close enough, stranger!" the stubby man said. "What the hell you creepin' up on me fer?"

"Who's creeping?" Slocum asked. "I came by to see if I could get some water."

The shotgun was an old model intended for hunting and was almost as long as the man holding it. "You got this whole damn river! Why you gotta stop right here?"

"That's a fancy setup you've got," Slocum said, pointing toward the modified wagon wheels. "Sifting for gold?"

"Gold or whatever I can find. What the hell business is it of yers?"

"So if I would have stopped farther down this river within sight of that wheel, you would have just let me pass?"

"So long as you didn't try touching any part of this stretch of river!" the stumpy man replied. "My claim gives me legal right of it from here to down by that eighth rock down there."

Rather than count rocks, Slocum shrugged and said, "Just thought I'd save you the trouble of chasing after me. Mind if I fill my canteen? If any chunks of gold fall in, I swear I'll hand 'em over."

The old man tried to maintain his scowl, but could only keep it in place for so long. "Fine. Take yer drink. Water your horse, while you're at it. No man would get nowhere without his horse."

"Amen to that."

Slocum led his horse to water and didn't have to make him drink. The stallion drank just fine on its own accord, lapping up the water as if it was trying to chew a hole through the bottom of the riverbed.

"So that's Shackley?" Slocum asked.

The miner still had his shotgun in hand, but was squatting down beside his wheel mechanism. "Last time I checked," he grumbled.

Reaching into his saddlebag as he stood by the horse, Slocum found his field glasses and put them to his eyes. As far as he could tell, Shackley was somewhat larger than the last few towns he'd visited, but was just as sleepy. Although a posse wasn't exactly an occupying army, he wasn't taking any chances by assuming the best. When he lowered the glasses, he found the miner glaring up at him.

"What you lookin' for?" the old man asked suspiciously. "You bein' chased or somethin'?"

Even though Slocum prided himself on having a good poker face, he felt his surprise come awfully close to the surface upon hearing that from the strange old man. "Chased? Why would you ask something like that?"

"Yer scoutin' that town like yer expectin' something from there. Maybe lookin' to avoid someone." After another couple seconds, the miner shrugged and began tugging at one of the spokes on the slowly turning wheel. "Ferget I said anything. When a man's been out here on his own fer so long, he starts jumpin' at shadows."

"Happens to the best of us. So, have you pulled anything but rocks from this river?"

The question had been innocent enough, but Slocum thought he'd stepped on the old man's toes by asking it. No sooner had the words come out of his mouth than the miner brought his shotgun up to his shoulder and sighted down the barrel. Slocum stepped back and raised his hands to chest level, but could still make a quick grab for his Colt if the old man pushed it that far.

"Someone's comin'," the miner snapped.

Upon closer inspection, Slocum could see the miner was aiming past him toward the trail leading to the river. "Are you expecting anyone?"

The miner looked at him as if Slocum had begun flapping his arms and clucking like a chicken. "Would I be pointin' my damned gun at someone I was expectin'?"

"I suppose not."

"What about you? Anyone ridin' with you?" Tightening his grip on his shotgun, the miner added, "You sure you ain't bein' chased?"

Before Slocum could think of a suitable lie, he saw the figure that had caught the miner's attention. It was a man on horseback, who'd come to a stop rather than come any closer to the river. The moment Slocum saw the glint of fading sunlight against something near the figure's eye level, he thought about two things: The man on horseback was looking at him through a telescope or held something else made of metal close to his face.

Acting on the side of caution, Slocum dropped down less than a second before the rifle shot cracked through the air. A single bullet tore through the space just above his head, and the miner answered back with a shot of his own.

"Get down, you damn fool!" Slocum shouted. "You can't hit anything that far away with a shotgun!"

"How do you know that?"

"How is it that you *don't* know that?"

The second rifle shot was taken hastily, but still tore up a patch of ground about four feet to Slocum's left. He drew his pistol and fired two shots in quick succession. He could tell neither of the shots would hit much of anything, but they gave the rifleman something to chew on for the next few moments.

"Who is that man?" the miner asked.

"He's the man trying to kill us," Slocum replied. "That's all I need to know. Now will you get behind something?"

Rather than heed Slocum's advice, the miner sighted down the barrel of his shotgun and pulled his trigger. The hunting rifle kicked against his shoulder and made a whole lot of noise, but the man on horseback was well beyond its range. Before the horseman could put the miner down, Slocum moved forward and fired another couple of shots at him.

When the man on horseback pulled his reins to move to another spot, the miner whooped and hollered. "Damn straight!" he shouted triumphantly. "Run if you know what's good for ya!"

Slocum walked up to grab the miner by the shoulder and pull him back toward the waterwheel. "Will you get back here before you get yourself killed?"

"What do you care if'n I get killed or not?"

"I was just asking myself the same thing."

Jamming the business end of the shotgun against Slocum's chest, the miner bared a set of rotten, crooked teeth and snarled, "Then let me be! This is still my damn claim!"

"Your gun's empty," he said as he shoved the man so the waterwheel was between him and the horseman. "That is, unless you rigged something to fix that situation." When he heard the clack of a hammer falling on a spent shell, Slocum said, "Didn't think so."

Suddenly, the old man looked around as if he'd just now figured out where he was standing. The rifleman in the distance fired another shot, which chipped away a chunk toward the top of the wheel. "Oh, no, you don't!" the miner howled. "I built this wheel! Ain't nobody gonna shoot her up!"

"Then stay right here and defend it!" Slocum told him.

"Don't think I won't!"

Slocum replaced his spent rounds with fresh ones from his gun belt. He didn't mind leaving the miner to guard the wheel simply because, if the rifleman got close enough to be hit by that shotgun, Slocum would either be dead or long gone.

The horseman rode toward the camp at a full gallop. Not

wanting to let the rifleman keep high ground and speed on his side, Slocum aimed and fired three quick shots at the rider. Sure enough, that was good enough to convince the horseman to veer to one side, pull back on his reins, and hop down from the saddle. He hit the ground hard, rolled toward a nearby log, and flipped on his belly to use that log for cover.

Slocum fired his remaining rounds into the log, hoping to drill through it and into the rifleman. Even if he didn't get so lucky, he was making enough noise to get the man's horse to keep running after its rider had jumped away. Unfortunately, that horse was either wild or loyal enough to charge directly toward Slocum. Waiting until he could see the horse turn to the right to avoid running into the stream, Slocum dived to the left to avoid getting trampled. That put him almost right back where he'd started.

"Real good plan you got there," the miner said from about three feet behind Slocum. "Looks like both you and that horse got yer heads screwed on the wrong way."

"You got a better idea?" Slocum grunted as he quickly reloaded the Colt.

"Yeah. Leave my damn camp and take that asshole with ya!"

"I got a better one. Give me that shotgun."

"Hell, no!" When the man behind the log fired a few wild shots toward the waterwheel, the miner gritted his teeth and flipped open a vest that was so dirty, it had blended almost seamlessly with his filthy shirt. Beneath the vest, tucked under his belt, were no fewer than four pistols of various models and sizes. He plucked out one of the newer ones and tossed it to Slocum. "Take this instead."

The pistol was another Colt, but a few years older than Slocum's. It had good balance, seemed to be in decent working order, and was much handier than the one he'd taken from Sheriff White and stashed in his saddlebag. "Don't mind if I do," he said with a grin. The pistol was loaded and ready to go, so Slocum decided to put it through its paces.

While running away from the waterwheel, Slocum fired toward the log with the older-model Colt. The pistol bucked against his palm, but felt as if it hadn't been fired in some time. Slocum could feel the difference in the trigger and the sound of the shot. It packed a wallop, but wasn't enough to flush the other man from where he was hiding. After firing a few more shots through the log, Slocum realized the other man wasn't even hiding there anymore.

The rifleman had worked his way around to flank the waterwheel, but only after Slocum had tried to flank him. All of this scurrying about resulted in a circular dance that kept each man from getting the drop on the other. Slocum caught a hint of motion from the corner of his eye, twisted in that direction, and fired his Colt Navy. Compared to the gun in his left hand, his own pistol sang while sending its smoky cargo toward its target. The rifleman fired back, but only as he leapt away from Slocum's line of fire. Those shots hissed close enough to Slocum's ear to get him to drop to the dirt, but didn't draw any blood.

"If you're trying to rob us, you're bound to be disappointed," Slocum shouted, "All we got here is a broken wheel and a bunch of rocks."

The miner crouched near that wheel, glaring at Slocum angrily until he realized he couldn't exactly refute the statement.

"Who says I'm here to rob anyone?" the rifleman hollered. "I'm after a wanted fugitive and known murderer."

As much as Slocum was hoping to hear something other than that, he wasn't too surprised by those words. The man had taken his first shots from afar, and fought like he was scared of getting his hands too dirty. If that didn't reek of a bounty hunter, Slocum didn't know what did.

"Which murderer is that?" Slocum asked.

"According to this notice, that'd be you, John Slocum."

Slocum swore under his breath.

"You're a murderer?" the miner asked. "I knew I should'a shot you on sight! Is there a reward?"

"Sure is," the rifleman shouted. "Shoot him now and I'll give you a cut."

"How much?"

"Gotta be more than what you're pullin' out of this stream with a broken wheel."

"It *ain't* broken!" the miner barked.

All this time, Slocum knew the rifleman was reloading his weapon and making whatever other preparations he needed to make before taking another run at him. But the rifleman wasn't the only one taking advantage of the lull in the fight. Slocum crept just far enough to spot the exact spot where the rifleman was hiding. Not only that, but Slocum had two weapons drawn and ready to go to work. The rifleman was using a pair of trees that had grown together to form something of a wall for cover. Once Slocum was close enough, he raised both pistols and let out a quick whistle.

The bounty hunter was no fool. At the first hint of an unexpected presence, he turned and fired. The rifle barked twice, and then a third time in a rapid staccato rhythm. Slocum kept the borrowed gun in his right hand and emptied it right away in a thunderous eruption. When the bounty hunter tried to shift to a better spot, Slocum switched his Colt Navy into his right hand and flipped the empty pistol into his left. When firing his own gun, Slocum took his time and aimed properly. The first few shots didn't hit the bounty hunter, but they chipped away at the trees he'd been hiding behind and forced him to keep moving. The moment Slocum had a clearer shot, he fired.

This time, he knew he'd hit the other man. Slocum could feel it the moment he pulled his trigger.

Suddenly, the bounty hunter leapt from his cover and rolled into some tall grass. Just as he was coming up to take a shot, he was hit by the spent revolver Slocum threw using his left hand. The distraction was just enough to affect his aim and send his next shot whipping past Slocum's right shoulder. The shot Slocum fired in return wasn't so wild, and tore a messy tunnel through the bounty hunter's ribs.

Instead of firing back or trying to roll in another direction, the bounty hunter let out a shrill whistle. This wasn't a mockery of the noise Slocum had made a few seconds ago, but served a similar purpose. This distraction, however, came in the form of a horse racing toward Slocum as if it had every intention of trampling him into the ground.

"Son of a bi—" was all Slocum could say before he threw his entire body out of the horse's path.

The horse thundered past like a train, shaking the ground every bit as much as a locomotive that had built up a head of steam. It skidded to a stop near the bounty hunter, and waited patiently for his next command.

Rather than try to pick out a proper target, Slocum fired a round in the other man's general vicinity. If he hit anything with that shot, it was because of divine intervention instead of skill. The answering shot from the bounty hunter's rifle was delayed a few seconds, which was all Slocum had been after in the first place.

"That'll be just about enough of this!" the miner hollered as he stomped forward. Before either of the other two men could say a word, the miner pulled one of the triggers of his shotgun. Fire erupted from the first barrel to send hot buckshot toward Slocum. Fortunately, Slocum was thinking straight enough to dive away from the incoming firestorm before any of the lead pellets found him.

The miner shifted his stance to aim at the bounty hunter, waited for that man to make a move, and then pulled his second trigger. The shotgun roared once again, keeping the bounty hunter from climbing into his saddle and digging a few small holes into his horse's backside. The horse reared up and pumped its front legs into the air, but had obviously only caught a small fraction of the shotgun's wrath.

The bounty hunter stood up just in time to catch a grazing shot from Slocum's Colt. Apparently, that was enough to convince him that the tide of the fight had definitely turned against him. Drawing a pistol using his left hand, he fired again and again while backing toward his frightened horse.

"Get down, you old coot!" Slocum grunted as he scrambled over to grab the miner around the legs and toss him to the dirt.

The older man kicked and cussed every inch of the way, but stayed down once the lead started to fly directly over him.

Slocum kept his belly flat against the earth, but stretched his arm up to return as much fire as he could.

The next few seconds felt and sounded like full-scale war. Lead scorched the air and the scent of burnt gunpowder coated every man's throat with grit. The old miner covered his head with both hands, and cursed Slocum and the bounty hunter in a series of profanities that were either muffled by his face being pressed against the ground or washed out by the gunshots. When Slocum felt the rumble of hooves against the earth, he knew the fight was over. Even so, he was more than a little cautious while lifting his head for a better look.

"Is he gone?" the miner asked while keeping his head down.

Slocum watched the bounty hunter ride away. The man didn't look back, and he sure didn't look as if he meant to slow down anytime soon. "Yeah. He's gone," said Slocum.

"Did I kill that horse?"

"What?"

"You heard me!" the miner griped as he struggled to climb to his feet. When Slocum offered a helping hand, the miner was quick to bat it away. "I didn't want to kill that horse while I was—"

"While you were shooting at everything that moved?" Slocum cut in.

"Not everything," the miner corrected. "I didn't intend on shooting no horse."

Slocum shook his head as he watched the old man stand up. All the while, he wasn't sure if he should try to help the old-timer or be ready to dodge a punch. "The horse was fine. Probably caught a few pellets in the rump, but nothing too serious. It ran away without a hitch."

"Good."

"You care to explain yourself?"

The miner looked at him defiantly. "I should ask you the same thing. If I knew you was wanted fer murder, I wouldn't have let you drink from my stretch of stream. Was that man right in what he said?"

"I didn't murder anyone," Slocum grunted as he studied the horizon to make sure the bounty hunter wasn't about to double back or circle around to take another couple shots at him. The man on horseback rode in an erratic line, but that was probably due to the horse fretting after catching the stray buckshot. That erratic line didn't, however, bring him anywhere close to firing range.

The miner didn't seem to want to fire at Slocum either. He didn't even bother reloading his shotgun before propping it against his tent and walking over to examine the waterwheel. The contraption still creaked as much as ever, and continued to slowly dredge up samples of the passing stream. "If you say you didn't murder anyone, I suppose I believe you."

"Well," Slocum sighed, "that was easy."

"Would you rather I believed you was a killer? I got plenty more guns, you know. Besides," he grudgingly added, "I saw all I needed to see when I fired at both o' you two."

Slocum reloaded his Colt, and spotted his own horse grazing about fifty yards away. The stallion might have been spooked by the gunfire, but hadn't bolted. Since the horse didn't seem intent on leaving, Slocum let it have its meal. "Perhaps you could explain that a bit for me," he said to the old man.

Grabbing hold of one of the paddles fixed between the wagon wheels, the old miner tugged at a section that had been splintered by one of the rifle rounds. Now that the wheel wasn't in motion, Slocum could see the wire mesh that made up most of the paddle. By the looks of it, the mesh was intended to catch bigger pieces that flowed through the stream, divert them into a small scoop at the bottom of the paddle, and let the rest of the water continue along. From where

Slocum was standing, it seemed that the only thing the wheel had caught was a whole lot of rocks and a few unlucky little fish.

"Simple," the miner grunted while he struggled to straighten some of the wire. "Guilty men run away when the odds turn against 'em. Leastways, a murderer sure as hell would run once he was outnumbered. A man tryin' to defend himself or someone else would stay put. You stayed put and that other bastard took off runnin'. Since he was the one to start shootin' in the first place, I guess I'll believe what you say over anything that comes from the other one's mouth. Also," he added while bending the wire to his satisfaction and allowing the wheel to turn again, "I don't never trust no one who offers money to do a dirty deed. That goes double once guns are skinned."

"You came up with this whole system on your own, huh?"

The miner looked over at Slocum and then back at his wheel. "Yep. Sure did."

Although it seemed to make some sense, the miner had also come up with an elaborate system of pulling random rocks from the river using old wagon wheels. Slocum decided that the old man might have been a little cracked, but his heart was in the right place.

"Thanks for your help," Slocum said as he extended a hand.

The miner slapped the hand away and walked to his tent. "Just get the hell off'a my claim."

8

Slocum rode into town as if he was walking on eggshells. He didn't want to ride too fast, in case he was headed into an ambush set by the bounty hunter from the miner's camp, or some other bounty hunter who'd tracked him down. But if he rode too slowly, Slocum might as well have stood at the end of a shooting gallery right among the clay pigeons. Even after settling on a good pace, Slocum never stopped looking over his shoulder.

Someone could have been ready to jump out from behind a rock, or they could have been lining up a shot from a hundred yards away. When Slocum finally made it into Shackley, he was ready to punch a hole into a wall out of sheer frustration. Unlike the last few towns he'd visited over the last several days, he didn't hunt down a saloon or a hot meal. Instead, he made his way to a quiet little boardinghouse at the end of a quiet little street. The last thing Slocum needed now that he was at the source of his most recent problems was to draw even more attention.

When he stepped through the door of the boardinghouse, Slocum let out a breath and grinned as if he'd just drawn three cards to fill a royal flush. Even with such happy thoughts running through his head, it took some work to make his smile convincing. The woman who stepped into the entryway to greet him seemed to accept the act just fine.

She was several inches shorter than Slocum, had a slender build, and wore a simple blue and white checkered dress that was buttoned all the way up to her neck. Light brown hair was tied into a braid that hung down just past her shoulders. Her rounded face was friendly, and she squinted at him as though she should have been wearing a pair of spectacles.

"Hello there," she said in a cordial tone. "Do you need to rent a room?"

Standing in front of her when she looked at him and smiled that way made Slocum feel as if he'd stepped into a warm beam of sunlight that had broken through an otherwise cloudy day. His own smile became easier to maintain, and he had no trouble taking the edge from his voice when he replied, "I do need a room. Hopefully, you're not all booked up."

"Not hardly. We rarely get boarders anymore. Most folks would rather stay at one of the hotels closer to the saloons." Suddenly, she covered her mouth with one hand as if she'd let a bad word slip in the middle of a church service. "Oh, my. I hope I didn't just talk you out of staying here."

"It'd take a lot more than that," Slocum replied earnestly.

"Good. Do you have a horse that needs to be put up? I've got a small livery in the back. It's clean and has an empty stall."

"Sold."

"Well, then," she added with a crooked smirk, "since you're in the buying mood, I've got some old saddles and some land that's all for sale as well." It wasn't two seconds before she giggled and waved toward Slocum. "I'm just kidding. That's terrible. Come on inside."

Her attempt at a joke wasn't the greatest, but she'd said it in such a way that it made him laugh all the same. Slocum stepped inside and pulled the door shut. The house had the genuine warmth of a home that ran all the way down to the foundation. The air was warm and smelled like cooked meals. None of the rugs or furniture was new, but they were all soft and worn in. For the most part, the house felt like a comfortable old sweater that wrapped around a man instead of simply being tossed on to keep a chill away.

"Is it just you here?" Slocum asked.

"Mostly. I have a caretaker who is usually within earshot, but I run the place. You'll just need the one room?"

"That's right. Unless you'd like to keep me company."

The woman's eyebrows rose for a moment as though she was close to taking him up on that offer. In that one second, she looked to be about eight years younger than Slocum's first guess. Either way, she was a far cry from a child and a long way from an old woman. That meant she was just right.

"That just wouldn't be proper," she said as if she only half meant it. "If you think this is that sort of place, then I'll have to ask you to leave."

"Fine," Slocum said without cracking a smile. "Can you point me toward the nearest cathouse?"

For a second, the woman looked surprised and confused. That moment passed quickly enough and she started giggling. "You're funny, M . . ."

"No mister for a nice lady such as yourself."

She'd arrived at a small desk in the next room. Circling around to stand behind it, she opened a book and scribbled some notes on the first page. Even though she didn't look up at him, Slocum could see the flush in her cheeks well enough. "You're a charmer, but I'll still need a name."

"It's Adam Clay." Although it didn't feel right to lie to such a friendly woman, Slocum didn't want the trouble connected to his real name to be dragged into her fine establishment.

"How long will you be staying?"

"At least a few days. Here," he said while putting down a few bills from one of the stacks of money Nellie had given him. "This should cover me for a while, right?"

Picking up the money as if she was afraid it might bite her, she replied, "More than enough. If you don't stay this long, I assure you I'll refund the difference."

"Don't worry about it, ma'am."

"Oh, please," she said. "My name's Lynn. If you like, you can call me that instead."

It had been a hell of a long day after a hell of a long ride. Before that, Slocum had spent a hell of a lot of time in a hell of a dirty cage. Even with all that taken into consideration, he didn't have any trouble smiling at Lynn and patting her hand. Her skin felt as soft and warm as he'd expected it to be. "Nice to make your acquaintance."

A few minutes ago, Slocum had been ready to tear another man apart. Now, he was on a leisurely tour of a boarding-house. The odd part was that he enjoyed that tour very much. The closest explanation he could think of was along the lines of how some folks said music soothed a savage beast. Slocum didn't need to explain it too much. He just appreciated the way Lynn soothed him. After the day he'd had, it was just what he needed.

When the short tour was over and Slocum was shown into his room, Lynn set a key on his dresser and asked, "Is there anything else I can get for you, Adam?"

"Do you serve meals here as well?" he asked.

"I wasn't expecting guests tonight, so there'll be no proper supper. I can make you sandwiches or something easy, though."

"Maybe I'll walk around, get a look at the town, and scrounge up some food on my own. It'd do me some good to stretch my legs."

"Then I can make you breakfast in the morning."

"Great. By the way, have you heard of the Chesterton Mining Company?"

"Of course. It's the biggest outfit in town."

"Do you know where I might find their offices?" Slocum asked. The instant he saw a question cross through Lynn's mind, he added, "I'm looking for work and I've heard they have some fine opportunities."

"Well, I don't know if they're hiring, but their office is right off of Third and Main. Big place. You can't miss it."

Just so that inquiry wasn't first and foremost in her mind when he left, Slocum asked, "Any good restaurants down that way?"

She rattled off a few suggestions, and then roped him into a conversation about what he might want for breakfast. He got the feeling that she would have talked to him for a lot longer, but he managed to pry himself away without being rude about it. Even so, he didn't want to leave so quickly. Lynn had the kind of face that any man could have looked at for hours on end. But Slocum wasn't just any man. He had a price on his head and it wouldn't go away unless he cut it off at the source. Apparently, that source was just off Third and Main.

Slocum wandered the town with his head down and his hands in his pockets. As much as he wanted to find the Chesterton Mining Company, march right in, and tell someone they'd made a huge mistake, he wasn't going to let his temper get the best of him. He'd come this far running roughshod, but he knew when it was time to rein it in. In the middle of open country, he could afford to advance and retreat. In a town that could very well be enemy territory, there were too many corners for him to get backed into. He found something to eat, and continued wandering down the shadowed streets.

Shackley was a comfortable mix of big and small. Some streets weren't much more than wide, well-worn trails bordered on either side by carts selling anything and everything anyone could want. The middle of the town was more like the strongest root of a tree. It was solid and much more established. The businesses there weren't about to be blown away by a stiff breeze like the tents Slocum had passed earlier. One of the businesses in particular stood like the anchor of the entire settlement. That was the Chesterton Mining Company.

The building stood two floors tall at its base, with an additional floor tacked on that looked more like a large attic. While the lower floors were both square foundations, that third floor was less than half the size of the other two and perched on top like a hat on a big, fat head. At this time of night, the mining company was obviously closed for business. The only light to be found was a weak flicker at the uppermost window. Apparently, someone was working late.

Slocum stuffed his hands into the pockets of his jacket so his holster couldn't be seen. As far as anyone else was concerned, he was just another fellow walking off a late supper. As if to test his theory, a pair of men walked down the street to come directly at him. Slocum lowered his eyes so he wasn't staring up at the top floor of the mining company, and casually looked over at the other men. He gave them a tired nod, being careful not to change his expression like a little boy who'd been caught with his hand in a cookie jar.

"Evenin'," one of the men said.

Slocum returned the greeting and began walking away. After a few steps, he glanced back to find the other two were already engrossed in their own conversation. Just to be safe, he waited until they were gone before walking back around to approach the mining company from another angle. Slocum could hear bawdy laughter and hollering coming from the other end of another street, so he figured that was where he would find the town's saloon district. Tucking that bit of knowledge into the back of his head, Slocum quickened his pace toward the shadows at the base of the mining company.

Once there, Slocum pressed his back to a wall and began circling the structure. He looked for windows, doors, alleys, alternate paths leading to or from the place, anything at all that he might need if things got too rough when he paid a visit to whoever had put the bounty on his head. Fortunately, the mining company wasn't a fortress.

When he rounded the corner to get around back of the building, Slocum nearly walked straight into a man carrying a rifle. The gunman stood with his back to the building, and immediately turned to look at the movement he must have spotted from the corner of his eye. The man brought the rifle to his shoulder and stalked toward the movement. Anyone out for a stroll, rifle or not, wouldn't give two licks about a bit of movement. They probably wouldn't have even known Slocum was there. This man was a guard.

The guard approached the corner of the building slowly and cautiously. He didn't twitch at every sound he heard, which meant he wasn't just some worker taking an extra salary pacing around at night. Narrowing down the area where the movement had come from, he hopped to the side so he could get a look around the corner without putting himself within an intruder's reach. If someone had a gun drawn, the guard would more than likely be able to fire first.

When the guard's finger tensed on his trigger, he realized he didn't have a target. The shadows were thick around that side of the building, since the torches lining that section of the street were a ways off and the moon was partially obscured by clouds. A tall fence surrounded the mining company, which cast shadows that might as well have been thick clouds of black ink.

The wind howled.

A bunch of drunks began singing loudly enough to be heard from one of the nearby saloons.

Some more folks walked along the street.

The guard stood in his spot, watching everything along the top of his rifle's barrel. Finally, he let out his breath in a tired chuckle and grumbled about needing to get some sleep. He lowered the rifle, walked along the fence and rounded the next corner to stride across the front of the building.

Slocum crouched within the shadow of the fence, watching the guard make his rounds. Slocum's hand rested on the grip of his holstered Colt, ready to draw and fire at the slightest provocation.

When the guard glanced back, Slocum swore the man looked straight at him.

He could feel a chill run down his spine, and knew the

guard had to have a similar uneasy feeling. And just when the guard seemed prepared to investigate the shadows further, he moved away. Just to be safe, Slocum stayed hunkered down for a little while longer.

Hearing the guard's footsteps slowly fade, Slocum got up and hurried to press his back against the wall of the mining company. From there, he followed several paces behind the guard so both men could circle the entire building. When the guard rounded the corner to return to his spot at the back of the building, Slocum broke off and headed for the street. Before taking three steps away from the mining company, Slocum spotted something that he'd missed on his arrival. Plastered to the front wall, there were enough wanted notices to cover a section of the building like cheap paint.

Although Slocum might have overlooked them at first, he recognized them well enough now. In fact, he wondered how he'd missed all those notices in the first place. Every last one of them was identical to the one Sheriff White had shown him back in McKalb. The only saving grace was the fact that there was no picture of Slocum for everyone to see. His name, however, stuck out like a sore thumb.

Slocum snatched one of the notices from the wall and walked away. The last half hour or so might have been tense, but hadn't been spent in vain. He now had a fairly good idea of the lay of the land. The light was still flickering at the top of the mining company building, but Slocum decided to let whoever it was get their work done.

Tomorrow was going to be a big day.

9

After seeing that first batch of notices, Slocum found more and more, until they seemed to be plastered all over town. On his way to one of the quieter saloons, he passed several more notices tacked to walls and hanging in windows, most of which were ripped, smudged, or in some other state of disrepair. At least, the locals seemed to be as sick of looking at the things as Slocum himself.

The beers he bought did a good job of taking the edge off, while still allowing Slocum to find his way back to the boardinghouse and stagger up the stairs. Lynn wasn't there to greet him, but he did see a dim light under one of the doors at the other end of the hallway from his own room. Slocum was too tired to pay his respects, so he just went to bed.

The next day, he woke up to the smell of frying bacon and fresh biscuits. By the time he pulled on a change of clothes and headed to the kitchen, there were some eggs being cooked as well. Lynn was dressed in a bright yellow dress and had matching ribbons tying back her hair. Instead of the braid from the day before, her hair flowed in soft waves down her back.

"Good morning, Adam," she said as she turned and showed him a smile that was brighter than her dress. "Did you sleep well?"

"Sure did. Mind if I have some of those eggs?"

"Help yourself to all of it. That's why I made it." She shrugged and added, "There aren't any other guests right now, so you get to be spoiled. Hope you don't mind."

Slocum pulled up a chair to a small table in the corner of the kitchen and said, "Mind? I feel like a king." Before he sat down, he was stopped by a sharp glare from his hostess. "What did I do?"

"Oh, nothing," she quickly said. "It's just that I . . ."

Following her eyes as they drifted away from him, Slocum spotted the place settings on the larger table in the next room. "Oh. Should I get comfortable in the other room?"

"There's fresh coffee out there," she said, as if she needed to tempt him further.

Slocum walked into the dining room. The table was decked out with a clean cloth, fancy dishes, and silverware that was polished to a bright gleam. As promised, a pot of coffee waited next to two dainty cups. Suddenly, Slocum felt peculiar about wearing his gun and hat. Although he took one off and set it on an empty chair, he left the other buckled around his waist.

He didn't have to wait long before Lynn came bustling out carrying a large bowl of eggs, a basket of biscuits, and a plate with thick strips of bacon on a tray. After she'd made up a generous plate for him, she clasped her hands and asked, "Anything else I can do for you?"

"Yeah," Slocum said. "Sit down and help me eat some of this."

Despite the hint of protest she tried to show, it was plain enough to Slocum that she'd been hoping to hear those very words. Lynn certainly didn't waste any time in pulling out another chair and sitting down. Fortunately, there just happened to be another place setting at that spot.

"You were out late last night," she said while pouring herself some coffee. "Not that I was keeping an eye on you, of course."

"Just out wandering. After riding, sometimes it's hard to sit still right away. Did you say you had another man working here to fix things and such?"

"Yes, but he's come and gone already. Without a lot of guests, there's not a lot of things getting broken."

"I'll try to keep my room in order."

The eggs were a little runny, but had some onions mixed in, which more than made up for it. "These biscuits are the best I've had in a long time," he said earnestly.

"Why, thank you."

"Say, have you heard anything about this reward that's been posted?" Even though he'd tried to broach the subject as delicately as he could, Slocum knew he might have sounded suspicious. Then again, he couldn't imagine discussing a bounty for the scalp of a murderer with someone like Lynn without forcing the subject. When she winced, he added, "There are notices all over town."

Her wince grew deeper and she scooped up some more eggs. "I know. It's rather disgraceful, if you ask me. Just because a Chesterton was killed, everyone who lives here has to hear about it. I'm more than willing to comfort a family in a time of need, but offering money for vengeance is just—"

"Unseemly," Slocum said.

"Yes," she said as if she was truly surprised to hear that word come from Slocum's lips. "It is unseemly. Even worse are the sorts of men that reward has brought into this town. Usually, the worst we have to deal with are rowdy miners. Now, professional killers are about. At least, whoever this murderer is had the good sense to leave."

Slocum nodded, stuffed his mouth full of bacon, and washed it down with a sip of coffee. "So, you said a Chesterton was killed. Who was it?"

"Patrick Chesterton. He's the son of the founder of the mining company and the brother of the current manager."

"How was he killed?"

For all the talk of it being unseemly, Lynn had no trouble diving into the grisly details. It seemed everyone liked a bit of gossip as long as they indulged behind closed doors. Leaning forward, she told him, "Some say it was for a gambling debt, but others think it was over a woman. I didn't know Patrick very well, but from what I saw, it was hard to believe he would get any woman he didn't have to pay for. The man was crude and obnoxious."

"Sounds like you knew him pretty well," Slocum chided.

"He stumbled by here one time at some ungodly hour, looking for a room. He stank of liquor and I would have turned him away immediately, but he is a Chesterton. Thankfully, before I had to let him in, some more filthy men came by to take him off my hands."

"Really?"

She nodded, enjoying the telling of her story almost as much as Slocum enjoyed his bacon. "He owed money to just about everyone in town at one time or another. Sometimes he paid it back. Sometimes he didn't."

"How did he get away with that?" Slocum asked.

"He's a Chesterton. Half the people in town work for that mining company, and the other half owe their living to it because they have to buy property from them or purchase building rights or Lord only knows what else."

Slocum never did like it when rich folks got their way just because of the size of their purses. More often than not, that led to the same rich folks stepping on others just so they wouldn't have to spend a few more pennies that they would never miss anyway. His resentment must have shown on his face, because Lynn was quick to try and comfort him.

"The Chestertons really aren't all that bad," she said. "They provide a lot of jobs and they are pretty easy to work with. It's just that Patrick Chesterton. He's no good."

"He *was* no good," Slocum corrected.

"Yes, I suppose. I don't miss him at all, but it's strange not to have him around."

Slocum shrugged. "Every village needs an idiot."

She grinned and raised her cup. "Yes, I suppose it does."

After breakfast, Slocum had intended to go to the Chesterton Mining Company to get to the bottom of the truth about that bounty. But the bits of gossip Lynn had served up along with her eggs and bacon seemed pretty interesting. While they might have gone well with his meal, Slocum had a sneaking suspicion he'd only gotten an appetizer. For the next course, he ventured out into town amid all the notices calling for his head on a platter.

It was amazing what a little rest, some good company, and a hearty meal could do for a man's outlook. Despite the fact that he was still wanted, Slocum strolled through the streets of Shackley as if he didn't have a care in the world. When he passed a row of those reward notices, he chuckled, pulled one down, and carried it into a saloon.

The Silver Nugget looked to be the sort of spot that catered to local miners. He kept his eyes open for any men who might pick his face out of a crowd, but didn't get his hopes up in that regard. Any self-respecting bounty hunter would have preferred a place with more bloodstains on the floorboards.

"Mornin'," grunted the tired man who tended bar. "Want some whiskey?"

"A bit early for that," Slocum pointed out.

"Fine. How about I pour it over some grits?"

It was impossible to tell if the bartender was offering some sort of strange breakfast special or if he was just being a smart-ass. His thick eyebrows remained low and the corners of his mouth didn't so much as twitch. Setting the notice on the bar, Slocum said, "Tell me what you know about Patrick Chesterton."

"If he's dead, I hope he stays that way."

"What do you mean *if* he's dead?"

"You heard me," the barkeep snapped. "Or maybe you didn't, since you still didn't pick up on the fact that you need to order somethin' before I kick your sorry ass outta my place." When Slocum slapped a few silver dollars onto the bar, the barkeep asked, "What'll it be?"

"Keep the whiskey and the grits. Just answer my questions."

Shrugging, the barkeep swept the money away with a deft gesture. "You a bounty hunter?"

"Who else would ask a question like that?"

"I suppose yer right. So you never met Trick?"

"No. Did you call him that because he was a friend of yours?"

"Nah," the barkeep replied. "If he was a friend, I would'a called him Pat. Since he lied like a rug to get out of paying for anything from a piece o' candy to a home, most folks call him Trick."

"Shifty one, was he?" Slocum asked.

"Couldn't believe a word outta his mouth."

"And you think he may not be dead?"

The barkeep pulled in a deep breath, held on to it, and glanced past Slocum before letting it out. One might even get the impression that he looked in the direction of the mining company before speaking ill of someone who was named Chesterton. "I don't know, because I ain't seen no body. If he was dead, I can think of at least a dozen men who would've drug Trick's worthless hide down the streets for all to see. Most of them's who didn't do the dragging would've cheered at the sight. The ones that were left are probably real new to Shackley."

"Who'd want to kill him?"

The bartender cracked a smile. "Me, for one. As for listin' the rest of 'em off, I ain't got time for that."

"If he is still kicking, where would he hide out?"

"A man don't get called Trick without him havin' a few up his sleeves."

"How much does he owe you?" Slocum asked.

That one caused the barkeep to stop and regard Slocum a bit harder. "Why would you ask such a thing?"

"Because perhaps I could get it back for you."

Narrowing his eyes, the barkeep asked, "And why would you do that?"

"If he's alive, there's gotta be a reason for him to want everyone to think he's dead." Tapping the notice, Slocum added, "And if he's alive, he's gotta be connected to this reward somehow. That means he must have this money laying around somewhere."

"He's a Chesterton. They all got money laying around."

"Which must ruffle your feathers even more that he won't pay off his debts."

"He don't pay because he knows he'll get an ass whipping from the men he's been cheating in this town." Although his hands remained busy wiping off the bar or rearranging the glasses, the barkeep's eyes remained fixed upon Slocum. "Maybe he is dead. From what I hear about this John Slocum character, he could'a killed Trick easy enough. Trick could shoot his mouth off better'n anyone, but he wasn't known for shooting much of anything else."

Slocum picked up the reward notice, held it in both hands, and studied it carefully. "I'm after a good payday," he said. "If this notice is to be believed, then I could get that by finding John Slocum. If Trick pulled the wool over this town's eyes, I figure I can get my reward by finding him instead."

"How so?"

Folding the notice up and tucking it into his pocket as if he couldn't step outside and find another couple dozen just like it, Slocum asked, "How much would you pay to get your hands on the man who went to such lengths just to get out of repaying his debt to you?"

"That'd just be more money out of my pocket."

"What if you pooled a few dollars with some more saloon owners or other men who are losing money by Trick going missing?"

The barkeep didn't respond to that right away, but Slocum knew he was hooked.

"That mining company is run by the Chestertons, right?" Slocum asked.

The barkeep nodded once. "Yeah."

"You think they might be hiding Trick?"

"Nah. They wouldn't see fit to pay off his debts, so why the hell would they go through all of this? Besides, there ain't a lot of that family left other than the sister, and she looked broken up about the news that Trick might be gone. Well . . . as broken up as anyone could be at the loss of an asshole like that."

"If I get ahold of him, you and some others around here could put together enough to make it worth my while to hand him over to you." Practically watching the wheels turn behind the barkeep's eyes, Slocum added, "You'd spend a little money to make back what you're owed. Plus, that'd send a hell of a message to anyone else thinking about forgetting their debts to you."

And just when it seemed the barkeep might not be on the hook after all, the man asked, "Would you need any of it up front?"

"Why don't you start by telling me anything you might know about where I might find him? Point me in the direction of anyone who could help and I'll see what I can scrape up. If it's anything that leads anywhere, I'll let you know and we can discuss fees."

"And what if Trick's just as dead as folks say he is?"

"Then you let me know where I might find this John Slocum fella and I'll cut out a finder's fee from the reward money."

Although the barkeep looked slightly confused, he'd heard just enough to keep his interest sparked. He blinked a few times, and then shook his head as if trying to rattle something loose that had gotten wedged in the corner of his brain. "Go see Elden down at Peeknee's."

"Where?"

"Peeknee's. It's a gambling den down the block. Mostly faro and a few wheels. Elden deals down there and he's owed a healthy sum by Trick. He might know a bit more'n me about where to find the bastard. He keeps his ear to the ground regarding most everything around here, so he may even know something about that Slocum fella. There's a few other places in a row near that spot. Stop into any one of 'em and ask about Trick. Someone'll have something to say."

Slocum nodded and placed his hands once more on the bar. This time, he leaned forward and locked eyes with the barkeep as if he was about to crawl down the other man's throat. "I don't suppose I have to tell you that if you decide to offer this same deal to some other bounty hunters just to see to it that Trick is found, you'll still owe me my money. And if you decide to change your mind after I flush out the bastard, and send some hired guns my way to take me out of the picture, I'll kill them and then I'll kill you."

The barkeep stepped back and raised his hands. "I was just spoutin' off. I don't know for certain that Trick is dead or otherwise."

Cocking his head a bit, Slocum added, "Or maybe you'd send word out to this Slocum fella to let him know I'm coming for him. You might think that'll earn you a pretty penny?"

"I don't know where he is," the barkeep whined as he waved his hands. "I was just talkin'!"

"How about you forget we had this little talk?"

"Fine! I don't care. If I can help, I'll help. All I want is my cut, just like you said." His eyes darted toward something beneath the bar, which Slocum figured had to be a weapon of some kind. Judging by the jolt of courage the barkeep got after seeing it, that weapon must have been something more than a pigsticker.

"If I do pull some money together, I want you to deliver Trick straight to me. You let any other Chesterton know about the arrangement and I'll see to it that you get strung up right beside me."

The barkeep's face went through more phases than the moon over an entire year. He started off confused, drifted toward frightened, inched into the angry territory, before circling back around and twitching in a few other directions. Finally, he collected himself enough to string together a few words. "I was just talkin' before."

"We still got our arrangement?" Slocum growled as he slapped his hand against his holstered Colt.

The barkeep nodded. While the few other customers in the place took notice, not one of them was about to step in.

"If Trick's alive, I wanna hear about it so I can bring him in," Slocum said.

"Yeah, sure."

"If Trick's dead, that means this Slocum fella must be around here somewhere. Right?"

"The hell if I know!"

Slocum cocked his head to one side and pulled his six-shooter an inch or so from its leather housing.

"I swear I don't know, you crazy bastard!" the barkeep sputtered. "But if I hear anything about it, I'll let you know."

"You'll tell me *exclusively*, right?"

Now, confusion drifted back across the barkeep's face. Slocum leaned forward, and used simpler words. "That means you'll tell me and nobody else."

"Oh . . . yeah. Sure. You and nobody else."

Slocum watched the barkeep for a few more seconds, but knew he didn't need to stay there much longer. He'd smelled fear plenty of times before, and this man reeked of it. Along with that fear, there was just enough confusion thanks to the liberal amounts of bullshit Slocum had sprinkled into his threats and bargains. The barkeep might not have followed Slocum's meandering business proposal, but he wasn't about to do anything to upset him. Even better, he seemed willing to be a source of information whether he understood why he was doing it or not.

"All right then," Slocum said with a nod. "I'll check back in on you in a while. Don't think I won't."

"I don't. I. . .I mean. . .I do. Or rather, I think you will. . .I think."

Allowing himself to grin, Slocum nodded. "That's what I like to hear." After that, Slocum was quick to leave. If he stayed another second, he ran the risk of laughing in the barkeep's face.

Even if Slocum had no intention of returning to that saloon, his visit there had been more than worth his while. He'd learned plenty while blowing smoke at that barkeep. For one thing, he knew he himself wasn't recognized in that part of town. Considering all the reward notices tacked up everywhere and all the bounty hunters that must have come through recently, that was saying a lot. He'd also learned a good deal about the man Slocum had supposedly killed. The mere fact that the barkeep made it known to a stranger that Trick might be alive lent some real credence to that possibility. No matter how much thinking Slocum had done during his brief stint in jail and the ride into Shackley, he hadn't thought the murder victim might actually not be a victim at all. The barkeep's theories might be awfully wobbly, but they were worth considering. Now he wanted to see if those theories held up. Fortunately, he knew just where to go.

Slocum's first stop was the saloon directly across the street. All he'd needed to do was drop Trick Chesterton's name to various men in there to get a scowl, a wince, a roll of the eyes, or all three. Gamblers and barkeeps alike didn't think much of Trick, and the working girls in the next few establishments had even more to say. None of it was good. Within the space of half an hour, Slocum had more than enough ammunition to take with him to the Chesterton Mining Company.

10

The first floor of the mining company was similar to a stock-yard. Several partitions sectioned off small spaces where business was conducted. Instead of cattle or hogs in those stalls, however, there were little desks where small groups of people haggled over claims, mineral rights, or job opportunities. Slocum couldn't pick up on many details, but he heard enough to know why this building was considered to be the financial center of this part of the Dakota Territory.

Within minutes of Slocum's arrival, he was greeted by a tall beanpole of a man dressed in dark trousers, a dark blue shirt with rolled-up sleeves, and a dark red vest. The man stepped up to him and asked, "What brings you to Chesterton Mining? Are you here about a job?"

"You might say that," Slocum replied.

"Are you looking to work the claim up north, or are you one of the men signing up for the eastern expedition into the hills?"

"Neither." With that, Slocum dug out the notice from his pocket and held it up.

The beanpole barely flinched. "Oh, I see. Have you found John Slocum?"

Resisting the urge to give a proper answer, Slocum replied, "I'd like to speak to the man who issued this notice."

"It was issued by the acting manager of this company."

"Then that's who I want to speak to."

"Your name?"

"Does it matter?"

The beanpole sighed and looked him up and down. Pausing for a moment when his eyes hit Slocum's gun belt, he clucked his tongue with disapproval. "You bounty hunters might make more progress if you tried working together a bit more. Maybe then you wouldn't have to be so deceitful."

"Is that a fact? Well, I'll take that under advisement. Now do I get to have a word with the manager or should I stuff a written message up your—"

"No need for all of that," the beanpole cut in. "I'll see if such a meeting is possible. Wait right here."

Slocum had to give the man credit. Even though he could have picked up that beanpole and tossed him like a horseshoe, he didn't seem to intimidate the scrawny businessman. That reflected either how many other bounty hunters had come through the building since the notices had been posted, or the beanpole's confidence in the mining company's enforcers. Slocum spotted a few armed men creeping in on him from a couple of different sides. Before the enforcers had a chance to earn their pay, the beanpole scuttled over to the narrow staircase he'd used a few scant moments ago.

"You want to speak with the company manager?" the beanpole asked. "Come with me."

Slocum followed the beanpole up the stairs. All the while, he kept his hand on the grip of his Colt. None of the notices had his likeness on them and nobody in town seemed to recognize him, but Slocum wasn't about to get sloppy. He made it to the second floor without getting picked off. In fact, everyone but the beanpole seemed to forget he was even there.

When he got to the third floor, Slocum was led past a short row of doors to the end of a hallway. Judging by the growing spaces between the doors, the rooms behind them were getting bigger the farther along they went.

Upon reaching the last door, the beanpole stopped, turned around, and held out one hand. "I'll have your gun," he said.

"The hell you will," Slocum replied.

"I won't allow you to march in there with a gun! None of the other bounty hunters had any qualms with obeying a simple rule, and if you have a problem, you're free to take it elsewhere."

Not only had the beanpole grown a spine, but he had some muscle to back it up. Just as he'd finished his huffing statement, a pair of burly men stomped into the hallway from one of the doors closer to the stairs. They had the rough look and sharp eyes of miners, but carried shotguns instead of picks and shovels. At the moment, they appeared to be more than ready to dig a few holes through Slocum's head.

Suddenly, the door the beanpole was guarding came open to reveal a tall woman with straight blond hair pulled back severely behind her head. "Is this the man you said you'd be bringing up here?" she asked.

"Yes, but he won't hand over his gun."

Shifting her eyes to Slocum, she asked, "Is that true?"

"Just being cautious, ma'am," Slocum replied.

After thinking it over for all of two seconds, the blond woman asked, "Do you have information regarding Patrick Chesterton?"

"I've stumbled across a few things."

"Fine. Come inside. The guards will keep an eye on you. If you so much as think about drawing that pistol, the first part of you to leave this office will be whatever's blown out through the window."

Those words sounded especially harsh coming from a face as pretty as hers. For some reason, though, Slocum was more intrigued than threatened by them. "Fair enough," he said.

By the time he walked into the office, both of the shotgun-wielding guards had moved up to within two paces behind him. Slocum didn't intend on skinning his Colt Navy, so he focused more of his attention on what was in front of him than what trailed along behind.

The office looked more like a study on one end and a library on the other. The first half was taken up by a crowded yet organized desk along with several smaller tables displaying maps and contracts of all sorts. The other half was lined with bookshelves filled with everything from leather-bound volumes to thick documents held together with tattered covers and loops of twine.

Turning to the beanpole, the blonde said, "I've got some other business to attend to. Why don't you come back in an hour or two?"

Slocum hadn't expected that.

After the beanpole left, Slocum stood quietly and waited for a few seconds. "You're the one running this outfit?" he asked when it became clear nobody other than the two guards was going to join them in that office.

Standing behind the desk, the blonde extended her hand and replied, "That's right. I'm Isabelle Chesterton. If you have a problem doing business with a woman, you can turn around and leave right now."

"I don't have a problem with it necessarily," he replied while shaking her hand. She had a strong grip, but not too strong. "It's just a mite peculiar to see someone like you in charge of so many men."

"Since my father and uncle passed away, I've had to defend myself plenty of times. I don't intend on explaining myself to a bounty hunter. Now, do you have something to say to me or not?"

"I do," Slocum said as he reached into his pocket for the reward notice. The moment his hand got to within a few inches of his gun belt, the guards tensed. Slocum could sense more fear in their eyes than anything else, but he played along as if he was just as nervous as the guards seemed to be. He eased the notice out and let it droop open.

Tossing a quick wave to the guards so they would ease up

a little, Isabelle asked, "So this has something to do with my brother?"

"Could be."

"I don't appreciate someone coming in to waste my time. Either speak to me directly or leave."

"I'd like to know why you're so certain that John Slocum killed him."

"There were witnesses."

"What witnesses?" Slocum asked.

"The same ones that saw my brother killed," Isabelle said.

"Were they friends of your brother's?"

"Yes."

"Good enough friends to lie for him?"

She let out a tired sigh and motioned for her guards to come closer. "Escort this man out of my office," she said. "And don't show anyone else up here unless you know for certain they've got real business to conduct."

Just as one of the guards grabbed his elbow, Slocum said, "I've heard that your brother may not even be dead."

"Where would you hear something like that?" Isabelle snapped in a tone of voice that was sharp enough to stop all the men in their tracks.

"I've heard speculation from folks right here in town," Slocum told her. "Folks that should have known if there was a burial or a body connected to the disappearance of such an important man."

"The fact that you call my brother an important man shows that you either don't know him or are mocking him. Either way," Isabelle pointed out, "I don't like it. As for any rumors of him being alive, they are just that. Rumors."

"So there was a funeral?"

"Yes."

"And a body?" Slocum asked.

Isabelle's eyes narrowed into angry slits. Considering the question, it was the sort of reaction Slocum would have expected from any sister who'd lost a brother. "That's a hell of a question to ask me."

"I don't mean to come up here and stir up trouble," Slocum said in what was a partial twist on the truth. "I just need to know what I'm dealing with. When you start calling in bounty hunters to go after a man like John Slocum, you're inviting plenty of trouble. With that many guns out and about, any job could get real messy. When I heard those rumors, it took me by surprise. That's all."

While Isabelle's anger seemed to have abated for the moment, it didn't recede completely. "If you want details regarding my brother's death, I don't have them. There's plenty about my brother's life that I'd rather not know. If you're looking for some information, however, you might want to try a faro dealer who works at an establishment called Peeknee's."

"Would his name be Elden by any chance?"

"Yes, it would."

"I've heard him mentioned before."

"That's splendid," she huffed. "It seems this whole conversation was a waste of time after all. I've posted my reward to see to it that my brother's killer comes to justice. If I'd wanted to play more of a part in that, I would have done so already. My guards have enough on their plate, and bounty hunters like yourself are more apt to find this murderer, so you go about it. I have more than enough to do with consolidating my family's business interests. If you have any questions, ask one of my managers on the first floor. Don't bother me again."

Slocum bristled at being called a bounty hunter, whether he'd been the one to get that ball rolling or not. Considering the low opinion he held of most every man who took up that profession, he had to admire the way Isabelle Chesterton handled the conversation. He tipped his hat and turned toward the door. When one of the guards attempted to grab his elbow to lead him toward the stairs, Slocum pulled free and continued along.

That guard was roughly the same height and weight as Slocum, but had a face covered in an uneven patch of whiskers that were probably intended to cover a large scar that cut across the side of his chin and ran down to his neck. The second guard was a huge fellow with a gut that hung over his belt and a chest that was bigger than most cider barrels. Unlike most fat men, he was solid and carried himself without gulping wind every other step. A thick, walrus-like mustache grew on his lip like an awning over a mouth that he seemed incapable of closing.

"Straight down and out the front door," the fat man grunted.

"I know where I'm going," Slocum replied as he stomped down the stairs.

When he was about halfway down the second staircase, the hairs on the back of Slocum's neck stood up, and he instinctively glanced back to find the fat man looming over that shoulder.

"Easy, Tad," the guard with the scar warned. "Miss Chesterton wanted him out. Nothin' more."

"Then maybe I'll do the rest for free."

"Just do what yer told," Scar snapped.

There were plenty of people conversing and wandering about on the first floor, but none of them took much notice of Slocum's armed procession. He took a few quick steps ahead, pivoted on his heels, and shifted so he moved sideways so that he could see where he was going while also watching the squabbling guards. "You two go on and have your little spat. I'll just see myself out."

The guards grumbled back and forth until Slocum was outside. The moment he shut the door behind him, Slocum dashed across the street and put his back to a post supporting the awning of a store that obviously catered to the sort of men looking for work from Chesterton Mining. Thanks to the front window where several shovels, picks, and pans were on display, Slocum didn't even have to turn around to watch the door he'd just used.

Just as he'd expected, the guards walked out of the mining company and glanced up and down the street. Having seen enough from the reflection, Slocum set into an easy walk before turning a corner. He quickened his pace, making sure to pass another long storefront with a wide window and then check the reflection. He didn't see either of the two guards, but he could feel some mighty heavy steps rattling the boardwalk behind him.

Despite not having been in town for long, Slocum knew the streets well enough to plot a course that suited his needs. Assuming he was being followed, he waited to hear the rattle of wagon wheels before turning sharply to cross the street. The nag pulling the wagon wasn't moving very fast, so nobody could have tagged along right behind Slocum without running into the wagon or being trampled by it. Once he was across, Slocum walked in a straight line that would keep that wagon between him and anyone in his wake. He hurried toward an alley and then turned back sharply.

After the wagon had rolled a bit farther down the street, Tad and Scar rushed across. They glanced back and forth wildly, quickly spotted the alley, and then placed their hands on their holstered pistols as they approached it. Walking cautiously forward, they continued to look back and forth to examine every possible spot where a man could hide along that narrow corridor. After a few steps, they moved faster to try and get to the end of the alley.

Slocum was panting a bit after running to the wagon, but his efforts had panned out. Not only had the guards missed the fact that Slocum had doubled back, but it looked as if the two men were going to chase a ghost all the way down the alley and possibly across town. Even if they came to their senses in another couple of seconds, Slocum would have changed direction yet again.

Peeknee's was easy to miss. It was a narrow storefront that didn't even look as big as the dress shop directly beside it. When Slocum stepped into the place, however, he discovered it was easily twice as long as any normal store or saloon. The back wall was almost out of sight, and just about every inch of the floor was taken up by card tables or a bar that ran just over three quarters of the building's length.

It didn't take much to spot the faro tables. They were longer and more crowded than the other games being conducted. At the moment, only two of those tables were being used. As Slocum walked toward the tables, he was singled out by the man who tended bar. Although he seemed ready to pester Slocum to buy a drink, the barkeep backed off quickly enough when he pegged Slocum as another sucker looking to buck the tiger. Content that his take of Slocum's losses would more than compensate him for the price of a drink, the barkeep went back to straightening his bottles.

The first table Slocum approached showed a hand being dealt by a gray-haired Mexican. Before Slocum could ask for any names, he heard the one he was after.

"Damn it, Elden, you got this table rigged!"

Slocum turned toward the second faro layout just in time to avoid catching an elbow in the ribs. The man who'd spouted off cocked his arm back to take a swing at the man seated in the dealer's chair. Before he could make his move against the dealer, the man was shoved away by one of the other gamblers.

"Sit your ass down and take yer losses like a man," the other player said. "Ain't nobody bein' cheated."

The man with the complaint nodded ferociously and said, "Sure! You just say that 'cause you're winnin'!"

"Exactly! I'm winnin' and I hate this son of a bitch. Ain't that right, Elden?"

The dealer wore a rumpled vest over a light blue shirt. Wide shoulders tapered down drastically, making him look more like a giant wedge as opposed to a man. He nodded, grinned, and said, "That's right. If I was gonna cheat in anyone's favor, it sure as hell wouldn't be yours."

"There! Satisfied?"

The complainer was either drunk or confused because he nodded and settled down, although he clearly didn't know why. "I. . .I guess."

Elden handled the cards awkwardly, but didn't have any trouble fanning them out and moving them around. The awkwardness was due to the fact that both hands were missing their little fingers.

Rather than announce himself right away, Slocum found a spot among the other men crowded around the table and played a few hands. Faro wasn't exactly his game, but he knew the basics well enough and even won a hand or two. More importantly, the rest of the players did a real good job of keeping Slocum from being spotted by anyone walking past or even through Peeknee's.

After an hour or so, Elden pushed away from the table and stood up. "I'll let George take over from here. Gotta stretch my legs."

Slocum drifted away from the table, along with a good portion of the other players. Rather than follow Elden outside and into the outhouse, he watched the side door until he spotted the dealer making his way back inside. Elden motioned toward the barkeep and took another couple of steps before he was intercepted.

"Mind if I have a word with you?" Slocum asked.

"Only if you wanna pay for the pleasure," Elden replied with a wry grin.

When the barkeep came over with a glass and a bottle of whiskey, Slocum took both from him and said, "My treat. Just bring over another glass."

The barkeep shrugged and went to fetch the glass.

"A word?" Elden grunted. "Hell, I would've settled for one drink. You split that bottle with me and you can have more'n a word."

The dealer walked with a pronounced limp as he led the way to one of the tables along the wall. Settling into his chair, he shook his empty glass impatiently. Only after Slocum filled it did he ask, "So what's on yer mind?"

"I'm told you might know a thing or two about Trick Chesterton."

"You lookin' to collect on one of his debts?"

"Not quite," Slocum replied.

"Then you must be one of them bounty hunters lookin' to find the man that shot ol' Trick."

"You're getting closer." Slocum paused and leaned back to take the glass being handed to him by the barkeep. By the time that glass was full, the barkeep had made himself scarce. Even so, Slocum lowered his voice when he said, "I noticed you didn't mention Trick was killed. Just that he was shot."

"What's the difference?"

"I've been shot plenty of times and here I sit. That's a real big difference."

Raising the glass to his lips and then tipping it back for a healthy swig, Elden studied Slocum carefully. "What're you after, mister?"

"I spoke to more than a few bartenders, cardplayers, and other men who didn't seem too surprised with the notion that Trick might not be as dead as everyone's letting on."

"Well, he didn't exactly earn a name like that by bein' straightforward."

"It also sounds like he'd weasel his way out of a lot of debt by making folks think he's six feet under."

"Yeah," Elden grunted as he downed another slurp of firewater. "He sure would."

Suddenly, Slocum caught sight of something moving directly behind Elden's shoulder. There wasn't anyone standing there, but something blocked the light passing through a knothole in the wall behind the dealer. Light footsteps tapped nearby, causing Slocum to tense.

"Relax, mister," Elden said. "It's just some lady trying on a new skirt." Seeing the confused expression on Slocum's face, he asked, "You ain't been here before?"

"Nope."

Elden chuckled and leaned with his elbows on the table. "This place used to be a storehouse or some such, but it didn't always used to be a saloon. It's always shared a wall with that fancy dress shop next door, though. Take a gander for yerself."

Slocum was expecting a few different things when he'd spotted that hint of movement. There was a chance someone had snuck up on him. There was a chance those two guards had tracked him down and were trying to launch a quick ambush. There was a chance that a stray cat was crawling along a windowsill. He hadn't expected to see a shapely woman's backside covered in nothing but bloomers. After a few seconds, that backside move away. The woman on the other side of the wall turned, placed her foot on a stool, and adjusted her stockings, giving Slocum a good view of her upper leg.

"I forget what this saloon used to be called," Elden whispered. "But men came in and asked to sit at the tables where they could peek at some knees. The more they asked for that, the more this place came to be known as the spot with the Peek Knee seats. After that, it was just Peek Knees."

"So the sign outside is spelled wrong?" Slocum asked.

"Nah. The ladies next door think we're a bunch'a loud drunks, but they don't know we're lookin' at 'em. Least, I don't think they know. No need to advertise, though. They might stop their little show."

Slocum leaned back to look at the hole in the wall rather than through it. It was tough for him to say whether the saloon's knotholes were a secret or not. In his years, he'd met just as many women who were too wrapped up in themselves to notice a thing like that as the ones who would have gotten a thrill out of being ogled while slipping in and out of their knickers.

"Trick liked this table," Elden said. "There's a redhead who buys an awful lot of dresses and takes a good long time tryin' them on."

"You heard from Trick lately?" Slocum asked. "His sister's awfully worried."

"His sister barely shed a tear at his funeral. Hell, she didn't even try to get a look inside the box where he was supposed to be spendin' the rest of eternity."

"Did she know the box was empty?"

Elden let out a sound that was half chuckle and half belch. "How'd you get a crazy notion like that in yer head?"

"I heard it enough times directly or indirectly for it to seem not so crazy."

"I believe it. Trick may be slippery, but he never was too good at keepin' a secret."

"So he is alive?"

Slowly, Elden nodded. "I saw him just the other day."

"So what's with all the reward notices and bounty hunters?"

"The reward's real enough. That sister of his may not be sentimental about Trick, but she sure as hell wants someone to answer for his death. Trick's downright touched by that. He wasn't so touched once the bounty hunters came along." Elden leaned forward on his elbows again. "But you ain't no bounty hunter."

"What makes you say that?" Slocum asked.

"Because you're askin' questions that would make a reward seem pretty damn ridiculous. Ain't no bounty hunter worth his salt that would cast doubt upon a reward bein' offered by a rich lady, no matter what he found out. Also, most bounty hunters I ever met were either arrogant pricks or loudmouthed assholes. So far, you don't strike me as either of them."

"Guess I shouldn't argue with that."

"Yeah, but that leaves me in a pickle. If you ain't a bounty hunter, then who the hell are you? A friend of Trick's would already know the answers to the questions you're asking."

"Not necessarily," Slocum pointed out.

"So who told you I'd know anything about Trick anyway?"

"Miss Chesterton for one."

Elden chuckled and poured some more whiskey. "Isabelle Chesterton is content to wash her hands of her brother any way she can. Even after I let her know I had somethin' to say about Trick's death, she never came to ask more about it. That bitch must have ice water runnin' through her veins."

"There were also a couple barkeeps who said Trick owed you a lot of money. If he's laying low somewhere, I could see to it that you get repaid."

"All of us?" Elden asked.

"He comes from a rich family," Slocum pointed out. "It's possible you could recoup a good portion of your losses."

"An' if he is dead?"

"Then you would have told me so a while ago and sent me on my way."

Elden smirked as if the lady on the other side of the wall had caught him peeking in at her. "You got a good point there. Trick does owe a good amount of money to a good amount of folks, but he's also got some other irons in the fire that I don't wanna even know about. Lately, he's been making some pretty rough friends. I wouldn't want to run afoul of them sort of killers."

"Then don't," Slocum said. "That's what I came here for."

"I may have heard some things, but it ain't much. A lot of men visit my table and they do a lot of talking under the proper circumstances. Let me see what else I can find, and come back tomorrow night."

"You could just tell me what you know right now so I can get started."

"Sure," Elden said. "But I got a feelin' that you might not wait long before tearing after whoever you set your sights on. There ain't no love lost between me and Trick, but I'd rather be certain I'm pointing you in the right direction."

As much as Slocum wanted to get a move on, he couldn't argue with Elden's logic. "Isn't there anything you can tell me now?"

"Trick told me he had somethin' cookin' to clear up all his debts," Elden said.

"When was that?"

"About two days before he was supposed to be shot dead. He told me to keep my mouth shut, so when I heard about the murder, it struck me as peculiar. He probably told some other saloon owners around here somethin' close to the same thing when he was pullin' together whoever he needed to do the job."

"That's what I wanted to hear!"

"And that," Elden said as he stabbed his finger at Slocum's chest, "is what I need to check on. I meant to look into that whole death and funeral thing on my own, but I'll move that up as well."

"What was holding you back before?"

The dealer flicked his eyebrows up and replied, "The money Trick owed me isn't supposed to be delivered until the end of the week. I got a letter to that effect a day after Trick was supposed to be meetin' his Maker."

"That is peculiar."

"Yeah," Elden said as he shifted in his seat to get another look through the knothole. "Ain't it just that?"

11

It had been a long day filled with a whole lot of walking. Slocum left Peeknee's late in the afternoon, but it felt closer to midnight. Clouds had rolled in from the west to cover the sun like a drab blanket, and a fine mist was spat onto his cheek by a brisk wind. Since he hadn't seen hide nor hair of those two guards from the Chesterton Mining Company, Slocum made his way back across town to the boardinghouse where he'd started his day.

Shackley was alive and kicking. Store owners either swept their stoops or bartered with customers at carts parked along the side of the street. Grizzled miners with stooped backs hauled pickaxes or shovels to surveyors' offices or to establishments advertising fair prices for gold or silver. The moment he caught sight of the boardinghouse, Slocum ignored everything else. All he could think about was getting some fresh coffee in his belly and a comfortable seat under his backside. He was so intent on getting those things that he almost missed the incoming fist aimed for his jaw.

The bit of motion coming from the corner of his left eye sparked Slocum's interest, so he turned to have a look. Seeing the punch being swung his way, Slocum snapped his head to one side, leaned back on his heel, and pivoted away from it. All of those motions came from nothing but reflex, and were enough to keep him from getting his clock cleaned. He still felt the painful tap of knuckles glancing across the lower portion of his face.

Slocum intended to defend himself as soon as he'd ducked away from that first punch, but since the punch had been thrown by the hulking guard known as Tad, it packed a little more wallop than he'd expected. His head snapped to one side quickly enough to throw him off balance. By the time Slocum recovered from that, another two men moved up to back Tad's play.

One of those men was Scar. The second was lean and wore a gun belt with a pistol hanging from one side and a large hunting knife from the other. His long hair was a light, sandy brown, which matched the finely manicured beard sprouting from his chin.

"You'd best have a real good reason for this," Slocum growled. Tad and Scar both rushed at Slocum with their shoulders lowered. Scar arrived first, so Slocum greeted him with a knee swiftly driven into his gut. The guard let out a pained wheeze and crumpled over. Before he could do anything else, Slocum dropped his Colt down like a hammer onto Scar's neck. The guard keeled over, clearing the way for Tad to swat at Slocum's gun with a pawlike hand.

Slocum managed to hang on to his Colt, but he wasn't strong enough to keep his arm from being knocked way out to one side. This gave the third guard a perfect opening to deliver an attack of his own.

"Shouldn't poke yer nose where it ain't wanted," the man with the light brown hair said as he buried his fist in Slocum's stomach.

Slocum tensed his muscles and let out a grunt as if the punch had hurt more than it truly had. A satisfied grin drifted onto the light-haired guard's face.

"Drop him to the dirt, Jervis!" Scar said as he pulled himself up.

Tad took a moment to chuckle as Jervis hit Slocum one more time. That was a mistake on the bigger man's part, simply because it allowed Slocum to catch his breath.

When he saw Jervis pull his arm back in preparation for another punch, Slocum lashed out with an uppercut that started all the way from his bootstraps and landed on Jervis's chin. The light-haired man spun on one heel and staggered away, sending a spray of blood from his nose into the air.

Tad swung a quick right at Slocum's nose, but wasn't quick enough for it to land. Slocum ducked under it, moved around behind Tad, and then wrapped his left arm around the other man's neck. Placing the barrel of his Colt against Tad's ear, Slocum said, "That's enough! What's the meaning of this?"

Scar and Jervis both had their guns drawn, but weren't confident enough to point them at Slocum. "You need to get the hell out of this town," Jervis said.

Pushing the Colt a bit harder against Tad's head, Slocum asked, "Would that be before or after I send this one to hell?"

As Scar tried to come up with the proper way to answer that, Jervis brought his gun up and fired a quick shot. The bullet hissed past Slocum's ear, but got more of a reaction from Tad.

"Hey!" the big man hollered as he squirmed to get away from Slocum. Now that he had something else to worry about other than Slocum's Colt, Tad was able to pull loose and join his partners.

Slocum had every opportunity needed to air out the big man's brains, but kept from doing so. In the time it took for Jervis and Scar to adjust their aim, Slocum picked out a target and pulled his trigger. His round clipped the edge of Scar's boot, which caused him to hop back a step.

Tad responded by turning as quickly as his lumpy body could manage, knocking Jervis aside with a thick arm, allowing Slocum's next round to whip through the spot that Jervis had previously occupied. Jervis kept his wits about him, and fired a few answering shots in quick succession.

Slocum dove for cover behind a post supporting the awning of a shop directly behind him. The instant his back touched the narrow piece of wood, he knew it wouldn't be enough to protect him so he turned and fired while hurrying into the store.

"There he goes!" Scar shouted. "Runnin' like a scalded dog!"

Replacing his spent rounds with fresh ones, Jervis snapped, "Don't just stand out here screaming. Get after him!"

"He's probably already gone," Tad said. "Just like the last time we chased him."

"Then don't let him get away. You circle round to the back of this place and we'll go in through the front." Jervis led the way as Scar moved in beside him and Tad ran around the store. The pair of guards held their guns at waist level and marched into the store like an invading army. They didn't make it more than a few steps inside before being stopped.

Slocum might have dashed into the store for cover, but he hadn't scurried away as the guards had thought. Instead, he'd picked a spot behind a shelf full of pots and pans and waited for another target to present itself. He had a clear shot, but waited for the two guards to realize the predicament they were in.

Apparently, Jervis was too stupid to fear for his life. He gritted his teeth, raised his pistol, and pulled his trigger. Scar followed suit, but took his shots more out of surprise and panic than anything else. Gunshots filled the little store and hot lead tore down the aisle. That commotion was quickly followed by the clang of bullets sparking against iron as several pans were knocked from their hooks.

Ducking behind the shelf, Slocum kept his head down until the gunfire let up. At the first pause, he knocked aside one of the pots hanging in front of him and returned fire. Scar caught that bullet in his upper arm and was spun around like a top. He screamed and grabbed at the wound, firing another wild shot into a pile of blankets to his left. Slocum shook his head as he watched the spectacle. Rather than finish the guards off, he leapt out from behind the shelf and fired a shot several inches above Jervis's head. The guard immediately dropped to the floor and tried to shoot back, but had already spent his last round.

"All right, dumb shits," Slocum said as he approached the two guards. "Time for you to tell me why you went through all this trouble to take a few shots at me."

Jervis was either not trying to hide the expectant grin on his face or was just doing a terrible job of it. Either way, it was plain to see that he was staring at something behind Slocum. Since the thump of heavy footsteps was clearer than the nervous muttering of the locals caught inside the shop during the fight, Slocum didn't need to turn around to guess what Jervis found so amusing. Instead, he grabbed one of the pans from the rack, twisted around, and flung it at the big fellow who had been trying to get the drop on him.

The pan hit Tad's face with a resounding *clang* and dropped to the floor. Tad wavered for a moment, but dropped to the floor about two seconds later.

Turning back around, Slocum said, "Now, about that explanation I wanted."

Scar tried to get up, but groaned and flopped onto his side.

Now that he was the only guard left standing, Jervis wasn't so brave. He also wasn't smirking. "We're just doing what we're told."

"Trying to kill me?"

"No!" Jervis squeaked. "Just scare you away."

"Who told you to do that? Miss Chesterton?"

After a slight pause and a wince, Jervis said, "Yes."

Slocum shook his head. "Try again."

Jervis's eyes widened as though he'd just witnessed a miracle, when the simple truth was that a blind man could have picked up on the uncertainty in the answer that had been offered to Slocum. "Somebody wants you out of town and I ain't telling you who. All you need to know is that if you don't scat, you'll—"

"Did Trick put you up to this?" Slocum asked.

Somehow, Jervis managed to open his eyes even wider. "How the hell did you know that?"

Slocum gripped the front of Jervis's shirt and pulled him close enough to whisper without being overheard by the store owner and customers who were starting to peek from their hiding places to see what had happened. "Tell Trick that I want to have a word with him and if he tries to skin out of town before I have it, I'll tell his sister all about his little plan."

Unlike Jervis, Slocum could cobble together a decent bluff. While he might not have been completely sure that Trick was alive until very recently, Slocum sure as hell didn't know about any plan a living dead man might want to put into motion.

"All right," Jervis said.

Slocum started to let Jervis go, but suddenly tightened his grip and added, "By the way. If you try to follow me or take another shot at me, I'll do a hell of a lot more than knock you around like I did here. Got that?"

"Yes."

"Where can I meet Trick?"

"He's got a cabin about half a mile away from town."

"Perfect." Just as he spotted the hint of a smirk at the corner of Jervis's mouth, Slocum added, "Better yet, I'll stop by the mining company tonight and lead him to a spot of my own choosing. Something tells me that'd turn out a lot better."

"He can't just wait around outside that place," Jervis sputtered.

"No, but he can hide like a little rodent, wait to catch sight of me, and scurry along behind me to the real meeting spot. Hasn't he been getting enough practice in that regard?"

Releasing Jervis, Slocum cast a disinterested glance toward Scar and headed for the door. He moved with an easy stride, and turned to walk down the street as if he was simply out to fill his lungs with some fresh air.

He didn't see any lawmen rushing to investigate the commotion or any brave citizens defending their boardwalk with a shotgun.

No panicked voices or hurried footsteps drifted through the air. When Slocum had left the store, Tad hadn't been moving enough to scrape so much as a fingernail against the floor.

The ground felt still beneath Slocum's boots.

Burnt gunpowder stuck to the inside of his nose and a hint of blood caked the back of his throat.

All in all, it was a fairly good end to an ambush.

Confident that his message would be delivered, Slocum took an indirect route back to the boardinghouse. Part of him hoped to catch those guards trying to follow him, just so he'd have an excuse to put those pricks down for good. Another part of him expected to be arrested by some fat lawman who'd been content to sit back, wait for the smoke to clear, and nab whoever walked away from the fracas. Both of those parts wound up being very disappointed, since Slocum made it all the way back to the boardinghouse without another incident.

He tried the door and couldn't get it open. Leaning toward the closest window, Slocum couldn't see past the frilly curtains Lynn had hung. Suddenly, the door swung open and a stout fellow waddled outside. The man dragged an oversized toolbox behind him and muttered in a language that Slocum guessed was German. Once the man had passed, Slocum went inside.

Lynn hurried from the kitchen, wiping her hands upon her apron. "Was that you trying the door? I hope you weren't standing there long."

"No, I just got here."

"Good. Well, come in. I hope you didn't get tangled up in that commotion down the street in the shopping district."

"I'm pretty sure I was right in the middle of that," he told her.

"Oh, my Lord! What happened?"

Rather than answer that question, Slocum came up with one of his own. "Do you have anything to drink?"

"You mean, like coffee? I could brew some."

"I mean like whiskey."

She winced and said, "Just a little. Sometimes I put it into my coffee."

"Then sure. Brew some."

"Only if you tell me about the commotion."

While Lynn brewed the coffee, Slocum told her a condensed version of what he'd done throughout his day. Although he skimmed through the conversation with Isabelle Chesterton, he found himself going through a lot more detail than he'd intended where the fight was concerned. That was most likely due to the fact that Lynn hung on every word, gasping at some parts and giggling at others. She was such a good audience that Slocum didn't even realize he was drinking coffee without a drop of liquor in it.

"So when you finished with those men, you just walked away?" she asked.

"Yeah. I was expecting to run into a little more trouble afterward, though. Doesn't this town have any law?"

"The Chesterton Mining Company took to hiring armed regulators to guard their claims and protect all the money that went in and out of their offices. They also pay more than the old sheriff could pay any deputies, so it wasn't long before the deputies switched sides. After the guards took to patrolling the streets and settling disputes between miners and most anyone else, nobody around here noticed when the sheriff stopped reporting for duty."

"So those guards are the town law?"

"More or less," Lynn replied with a shrug.

"Great. That's just great. Where's that whiskey you promised?"

She fished into a cupboard for the bottle as if she was digging for a stash of stolen gold. After pouring a nip of liquor into Slocum's cup, she put a little into her own as well. "I wouldn't worry too much about tussling with those men," she said. "No matter what they do around here, they're not the law. Did anyone step in on their behalf during all the shooting?"

"Not really."

"That's because everyone knows those guards are just men with big mouths and guns. It just so happens that they keep some semblance of peace in Shackley, but that's only because it's in the best interests of the mining company. More often than not, they just swagger and expect to be treated like kings. I'll bet the owner of that store with all the pots and pans is probably telling everyone he knows about how you whipped those three right in front of him."

Slocum sipped his coffee. It tasted great and the whiskey was stronger than he'd been expecting. Either that, or the liquor had just burned past some of his recently bruised innards. Within moments, he felt Lynn's hands start rubbing against his chest.

"Are you hurt?" she asked. "All this talk about fighting and I never even bothered to ask that."

"I'm fine."

"I suppose a bounty hunter is used to being in fights?"

"Yeah. You might say that." It still grated on Slocum to lie to her, but it wasn't exactly a good idea to mention his real name when it was the same as the name plastered all over town along with words like "murderer" and "reward."

"Why were those Chesterton men after you anyway?" she asked.

Instead of answering that question, Slocum placed his hand on Lynn's and held it firmly against the muscle over his heart. "Never mind about that," he said.

She squirmed a little, but didn't try to pull away. Instead, Lynn seemed to be flustered by just how much she didn't want to take her hand away from Slocum's chest. "Were those men trying to protect whoever killed Patrick Chesterton?" she asked.

"Do you really want to talk about this anymore?"

"It's all anyone in this town has been gossiping about."

Lynn's body was warm and she smelled like a fresh breeze. Since she was close enough for Slocum to enjoy all of that, he found his thoughts drifting farther away from gossip or anything regarding Trick Chesterton. Since nobody had followed Slocum this far and those guards were undoubtedly licking their wounds right about now, he knew he had a bit of time before the next storm.

"How'd you like to start some scandal of your own?" he asked.

12

No more boarders had checked into the house since Slocum had last been there. With the stout worker already gone, that only left Lynn and Slocum inside the place. Even so, she lowered her eyes and voice as she allowed herself to be led toward the stairs.

"What's the matter?" Slocum asked.

"Nothing."

"You're awfully quiet."

She looked around and whispered "Someone may come in."

"Are you expecting anyone?"

"No," she replied while passing the front door. "But I'm still open for business. What if someone wants to rent a room?"

Slocum reached out to lock the front door. "There. Problem solved."

Lynn stared at the windows beside the door and studied the shadows moving behind the curtains. As Slocum touched her face, she pulled back with a quick gasp. He kissed her gently at first, lingering until he felt her tensed muscles begin to relax. When he wrapped his arms around her and pulled

her close, Lynn practically melted against him. She leaned
back to catch her breath, but also let out a moan that built
into something that shook her entire body.

Slocum meant to take her upstairs to his bed, but didn't
even make it up two steps before she tugged at his shirt and
kissed him again. Lynn's mouth urgently mashed against his
as her hands greedily moved over his bare back and stomach.
She wasn't trying to grab him so much as she was simply
touching any part of him she could reach. Slocum could
sense that she'd been attracted to him, but even he was surprised by what he'd unleashed.

"God, yes," she sighed once Slocum reached around to
grab her backside. Lynn wrapped her arms around his neck
and stood one step higher than he did. That way, she was
raised almost exactly to Slocum's height.

Placing one foot on the step where Lynn stood, Slocum
pulled her skirts up and reached beneath them to find her
soft, smooth skin. Lynn used one arm to brace herself against
the wall, and gripped the banister with her other hand. As
Slocum moved his hands up farther along her thighs, she
leaned her head back and let out a breath that might have
been building inside her since Slocum had first walked
through her door.

She wasn't wearing much beneath her skirts, so it took
very little effort for Slocum to pull aside her underthings and
slip a hand through the downy thatch of hair between her
legs. Lynn's eyes snapped open and she tightened her grip
upon the banister as if she was about to yank it loose.

"Oh, my Lord," she moaned as Slocum's fingers played
along the moist lips of her pussy. When his fingers slipped
inside her, she couldn't form any words whatsoever.

Slocum enjoyed the warm dampness between her thighs,
but he truly savored Lynn's reaction to every little move he
made. Just watching her squirm and writhe was enough to
get him hard. When he brushed the side of his hand against
the inside of her thigh, Lynn spread her legs open a bit
more for him. While he slowly eased his fingers in and out

of her, she trembled with a quick burst of a few short climaxes.

Lynn looked at him the way a hungry predator eyes its prey. Slocum didn't need to hear or see one more thing. He took his hand out from beneath her skirts, and was immediately grabbed around the wrist. She then moved his hand up to her mouth and ran her tongue along his fingers to taste her own sweet juices. Slocum hadn't expected that, but it was one hell of a pleasant surprise.

Unable to wait another second, he picked her up and set her down again so she was sitting on the edge of a stair. As Slocum unbuckled his belt, Lynn reached out to pull his jeans down. The moment she got a look at his rigid cock, she wrapped her hands around it and began stroking. Now it was Slocum's turn to grab the banister for balance.

At first, it felt good enough to have a woman's hands on him. She stroked and cupped him daintily at first, but quickly built to a more vigorous rhythm. Lynn instinctively leaned forward and opened her mouth, but stopped short of letting him pass between her lips. Looking up at him, she slowly worked her hands between his legs.

"Don't stop now," he told her. "You're doing just fine."

Slowly, Lynn opened her mouth and leaned forward. His shaft was rock hard and aching by now. When he finally felt Lynn's lips wrap around the tip of his rigid pole, Slocum thought he might burst. Just when it seemed she might change her mind, Lynn practically devoured his cock. She slid her lips all the way down to its base and then started bobbing her head back and forth. It wasn't long before she got comfortable enough to suck him in long, lingering strokes. Soon, she reached around to grab his hips and enjoy every last inch of him.

As much as Slocum would have liked to let her keep going, there were plenty of other things he wanted to do. He tried easing her back, but Lynn was too absorbed in what she was doing to be deterred so easily. Eventually, Slocum had to push her away while easing his hips away from her mouth.

She looked up at him with wet lips and wide, disappointed eyes.

"Did I do something wrong?" she asked.

"Not hardly. Time for you to lay back and let me do some work."

She did as she was told, positioning herself as best she could despite the angle of the stairs against her hips and shoulders. Before she had a chance to think about her discomfort, Slocum was bunching her skirts up around her waist and settling his face in between her legs. At the first touch of his tongue against her wet pussy, she arched her back, propped one foot against the stairs, and draped the other leg over Slocum's shoulder.

"Oh, my God," she groaned. Wriggling in a way that complemented the motion of Slocum's mouth against her, Lynn used the foot resting against Slocum's back to pull him in closer.

It took some effort to pull free of Lynn's strong legs, but Slocum did just that so he could crawl a bit higher along the stairs. He kicked off his jeans, settled in between her legs, and guided his cock to her glistening pussy. Lynn was so wrapped up in the pleasure she'd felt before that she was startled by the feel of him entering her. She pulled in a sharp breath, grabbed the back of his neck, and propped her foot solidly against one of the posts supporting the banister.

Slocum plunged all the way into her. He pulled out an inch or so, slipping his hands under her to grasp her buttocks. From there, he lifted her up and off the stairs just enough to pump in and out of her a little easier. Lynn accommodated him every step of the way. Lifting her backside up while spreading her legs, she made it that much easier for Slocum to use the angle of those stairs to his advantage.

Just as both of their bodies found a perfect rhythm, someone knocked on the door.

"What?" Lynn gasped. "Did you hear that?"

"Forget it," Slocum said as he continued to move in and out of her. "I locked the door. Don't worry."

"Ed's got a key. So does Margie. What if it's one of them?"

Slocum didn't know who either of those people were and he didn't care. As far as he was concerned, the President of the United States and the Queen of England could both wait outside until he was through.

The knock came again. This time, it was stretched out into a prolonged series of bangs that rattled one of the windows in its frame.

"I'd better see who it is," Lynn whispered.

"Are you expecting anyone?"

"No."

"Then they can wait," Slocum told her.

Suddenly, a figure cast a shadow on one of the curtains covering the front window and a muffled voice asked, "Anyone in there?"

"Might be a customer," Lynn said. "I should probably—"

Slocum stopped her in mid-sentence by easing all the way into her. Lynn's backside felt good in his hands. The upper portion of her dress was askew and the lower half of her body was bare and sweaty. That, combined with the fact that every part of her was tense and trembling, made Slocum's erection almost too hard to bear.

"That may be Hank. He's got a key, too," she said. "I should really— "

"You should really what?" Slocum asked as he slid out and then buried his thick shaft inside her. He must have hit a sweet spot, because Lynn suddenly forgot about who might be knocking on the door.

She wrapped both arms around him and kissed him with renewed passion. As Slocum moved like a piston between her legs, she chewed on his lips and slipped her tongue into his mouth. Every time the person at the door knocked, Lynn moaned softly and ground herself harder against Slocum's body.

Eventually, the slope and edges of the stairs were more trouble than they were worth. Slocum got up and helped

Lynn to her feet so they could climb the rest of the way to the second floor and get to a proper bed. She, however, had other plans. The moment Lynn got to the top of the stairs, she grabbed onto the uppermost edge of the rail with both hands.

"What are you doing?" Slocum asked.

But all he needed to do was look at her to get the answer to that question. Lynn stood with her legs a shoulder-width apart and her backside pointed his way. Looking over her shoulder at him, she grinned and wiggled her rump invitingly.

Slocum wasted no time in stepping behind her, hiking up her skirts, and rubbing the soft flesh of her buttocks. Placing one hand on her waist, he guided his rigid cock into her and pushed his hips forward. Lynn grabbed the rail and lowered her head as she accepted him inside her. Letting out a throaty moan, she snapped her head up to look toward the front door. There was still a bit of movement from the porch, but she was no longer concerned about it. In fact, Lynn giggled like a naughty little girl while Slocum continued to make her feel like the only real woman in town.

He could feel another climax work its way through her body. The series of little trembles was unmistakable, but Slocum continued pumping until they subsided. When it seemed as if Lynn no longer had the strength to remain upright, he gripped her hips even tighter and thrust with even more vigor. Every time he pulled back, it was as far as he could go without slipping from her moist embrace. And every time he thrust forward, it was to bury his pole into her as deep as it would go. Lynn sighed under her breath every time his hips bumped against her. When she turned to look back at him, she watched his face until he closed his eyes to savor a powerful orgasm.

Slocum drove into her one last time and stayed there. After a few seconds, he exhaled. As if pouncing on an opportunity, Lynn pushed herself back against him and wriggled her backside until he started to grow hard once again. She squirmed and writhed until Slocum finally had to take a step back.

"You're gonna make it so I won't be able to walk another step," he said.

Still looking over her shoulder, she reached back to hold her skirts up and offer herself to him. "Why's that so bad? You goin' somewhere?"

"Thought I might go to my room and get a real mattress under me."

"How about I show you the rest of the house? There's plenty of other rooms for us to break in."

Slocum took her up on her offer, but only after insisting she check to make sure all the doors were locked and all the windows were covered. At least that way, he bought himself some time to catch his second wind. He needed it . . . right along with a third and fourth wind.

Lynn didn't tire out for a good long while. Even after they were both spent, she rested for an hour or so before getting up and tending to her chores. She bustled from one spot to another, picking up steam while whistling or humming to herself. As she approached the front door, she absently tugged at the collar of her dress to make certain that all her buttons were properly fastened. Giggling as she cast a quick glance toward the staircase, she pulled the curtains aside to take a peek at her porch.

The only thing she could see out there was a scruffy dog sniffing at a spot of well-tended flowers. Before the mutt could drop a present into that flowerbed, Lynn pulled the door open and hissed, "Go on now. Shoo!"

"Hope you're not talking to me," said a thin man who stepped onto the path leading to her front door.

Lynn jumped with a start and instinctively grabbed for the door handle. Pressing one hand to her heart, she said, "You frightened me."

"Sorry about that, ma'am. I came by earlier and knocked, but nobody answered."

"Oh," she replied as color flushed into her cheeks. "I must have been busy. Do you need to rent a room?"

"I just have some questions to ask, but I'm willing to pay you for your time." With that, he reached into his shirt pocket and produced a small bundle of money. When she didn't respond right away, he added, "If this isn't enough to make it worth your while, I can remedy that. How much would it be to rent one of your rooms?"

"What questions do you want to ask?"

"I'd like to know about the man who's staying here. What can you tell me?"

Slocum watched all of this from the top of the stairs. He'd gotten a little rest after working up a sweat with Lynn, but the sight of the visitor on the front porch got him up and moving. In fact, it took a good deal of effort to rein himself in after recognizing the man who'd ambushed him at that waterwheel outside of town. For the moment, it appeared as if the man didn't know Slocum was near. If he made one move toward Lynn, however, Slocum was ready to burn him down.

"There's not much for me to say," she said. "He needed a room and I rented him one."

"Is he here?"

"No. I don't know where he went."

Even from where Slocum was crouched, he could tell she was lying. Deciding that the other man could tell that just as well, Slocum eased his fingers around the grip of his Colt and prepared himself to fire a quick shot.

"Do you expect to see him soon?" the other man asked.

"I can't say for certain," Lynn replied. "Probably."

"What time should I try back?"

"Whenever you like. If you'd prefer to rent a room, I've got plenty."

Slocum gritted his teeth when he heard that. While those words made it seem as though Lynn truly had nothing to hide, they could backfire all too easily.

The man at the door shifted on his feet and leaned inside. Slocum backed up before he was spotted, and pressed his shoulders against a small table situated at the top of the stairs.

"Yeah," the man said. "I think I would like to rent a room."

"Damn it," Slocum grunted under his breath.

Lynn placed her hand on the door frame to keep the man from entering. "Is that your horse outside?"

"Yes, it is."

"Bring it around back. I've got a small stable there and you're welcome to a stall. Also, I'll need your name."

"My name?"

"That's right," she said. "For the register. By the time you come inside, I'll have you all written into my book and ready to go."

After a pause, the man told her, "My name's Duvall. Is that enough for your book?"

"Yes, sir."

Duvall attempted to poke his head inside once more, but Lynn held her ground. He turned and walked away as Lynn shut the door. After peeking through the front window for a few seconds, she spun around and lifted her skirts just enough to clear her feet as she raced up the stairs.

Standing up to meet her, Slocum growled, "What the hell did you do all that for?"

"His name is Duvall. Do you know him?"

"Yeah, I know him! He tried to kill me outside of town. Now, since we'll be bunking right down the hall from each other, I'll probably get to know him a lot better."

"What would you have me do?" she snapped. "He was suspicious and trying to get inside. If I didn't say what I did, he would have known I was hiding something."

"Did you have to offer him a room?"

"He didn't want to rent a room! I make my living from knowing when someone is ready to spend any money or not, and he wasn't intending on staying here. I thought I would just act like nothing was wrong and he would move along. I didn't think he'd take me up on my offer."

Slocum reminded himself that Lynn probably wasn't accustomed to dealing with gunmen or giving shelter to fugitives. It seemed she'd done the best she could after being caught off her guard.

"Maybe he's not even after you," she said.

"I can't take that chance," Slocum replied as he pulled on his boots and collected a few other things.

"Why would a man be after you anyway? Is it anything to do with that bounty?"

"No time to explain," Slocum told her.

"You should still have another minute or two. The latch on that stable is tricky and he'll have to get to the stall all the way in back because—"

"Because my horse is in there!" Slocum cut in. "Damn it all to hell. He might recognize my horse!"

All of the color drained from Lynn's face as she asked, "Is there going to be trouble here?"

"No, because I'm leaving."

"Should I distract him?"

Taking her face in his hand, Slocum looked into her eyes to find a mix of fear, panic, and worry. He leaned forward and kissed her. It was quick, but more than enough to put at least some of those fears to rest. She would have continued the kiss longer if Slocum hadn't pulled away. "I'll hop out this window," he said. "Don't worry about a thing."

"What should I do when he comes back? Are you leaving me alone with him?"

"I won't go far. Just tell him whatever he wants to know. Bring him up here if he asks. Don't lie and don't do anything foolish. He's not after you, so he shouldn't do anything if you don't provoke him. I'll see to that."

That allowed her to draw an easier breath, but the panic in her eyes returned when the sound of the front door opening drifted up from the first floor.

"Go on and tend to him," he said. "Just don't care for him like you cared for me."

"I don't care for every man like that!"

Slocum was glad to see the spark in her eyes flare up enough to make her look more like her normal self. Leaving her with that spark, he pushed open the window that led from his room to the steep slope of the house's roof. He'd barely pulled his fingers away from the sill before Lynn shut the window and pulled it tight.

Before she could leave the room, Slocum tapped on the glass to catch her attention. Lynn turned and waved viciously at him, but he tapped some more until she came back.

Opening the window a crack, she whispered, "He's downstairs. Just go!"

"Remember what I said. Just tell him whatever he wants to know. He's dangerous."

"Fine. Now go."

Slocum stayed at the window and watched Lynn hurry out of the room. From where he was outside, he could see her turn toward the stairs, and could also hear what was going on at the front door just below him. Duvall must have been taking a peek outside, but he'd closed the door again by the time Lynn would have made it down the stairs.

The roof was steep, but Slocum was able to find footholds on the shingled surface. He crouched and shuffled down an inch or two, which made a dry scraping sound that was loud enough to roll through the early evening air.

13

"Sounds like you've got company," Duvall said.

Lynn came down the stairs, rubbing her hands together and then wiping them on her skirt. "Not at all. I was just getting your room situated."

"What was all that noise?"

"I dropped a box of silverware," was the first thing she thought to say. Seeing the question brewing in the man's head, she added, "I keep the good silver upstairs. It's been a while since I've had many guests, so I thought I'd give you boys the royal treatment." She topped it off with a wide smile that wasn't quite as warm as the ones she'd shown Slocum.

"There was another horse in the stable."

"I told you there was another guest."

"What's his name again?"

Reluctantly, Lynn replied, "I don't recall."

Duvall strode forward in a way that made it clear he wasn't about to be stopped. Lynn did try to step in front of him, but he pushed her aside with relative ease. The moment he got to her little desk, he grabbed the register and read it. "Adam Clay, huh? You sure about that?"

"That's what he signed."

"I thought you said you were going to put my name in here as well."

"Oh, I guess I got sidetracked."

"Right. With the silverware," Duvall grumbled. "Where is that silver anyway?"

Lynn pulled in a deep breath and let it out harshly. Crossing her arms, she cocked her head and glared at him. "If you don't want to stay here, you can leave. This is my place and I haven't done anything wrong. I don't need to stand here and be spoken to in such a gruff manner."

Duvall nodded, grinned, and propped his rifle on the edge of the desk. The weapon had been held down against his leg before, but now he obviously wanted it to be seen. "You're right. I apologize. Normally, I only speak so rudely to folks who I know are lying to me. That wouldn't be the case here, would it?"

"What would I lie about?"

"The other man that's staying here for one. His name ain't Adam Clay."

"Isn't it?"

"I think you already knew as much."

She twitched and shook her head. "He rented a room, paid in advance, and hasn't caused any trouble. You, on the other hand, come in here waving your rifle around and accuse me of lying. Which of you two should I favor right now?"

"I suppose you're right." Without batting an eye, Duvall added, "Do you know the man renting your other room is a killer?"

"What?"

The surprise on her face was genuine enough and Duvall could see it. He even took some of the edge from his own voice when he said, "Maybe you didn't. How about you tell me where he is."

"I don't know where he is."

"Did he pay you to cover his tracks?"

"No," Lynn replied.

"Is he here?"

"No!"

Now that the fire returned to her eyes, Duvall responded in kind. He stepped forward as if he meant to shove her out through the front door. "Are you a friend of his? Considering all the notices tacked up around this town, it's a wonder that anyone here would protect John Slocum."

"I didn't tack up those notices," she pointed out. "I just live here."

Duvall's fist sliced past her face to slam against the closest wall. Lynn cowered and instinctively covered her head with both arms. "If you're hiding a killer, I got every right to tear this place apart looking for him. If you stop me, you're just aiding a criminal!"

"I don't know anything else. I swear it! He's not John Slocum!"

Grabbing her by the hair, Duvall forced her to stand upright. "Take me to his room."

"Why?"

"Just do it!"

Lynn was too frightened to do anything other than what Duvall had ordered. When she began climbing the stairs, he let go of her hair. Before she got all the way to the top, however, she felt the touch of cold iron against the small of her back. "You don't need a gun," she said. "I'll take you to Mr. Clay's room."

"I know you will. The gun's just to let you know I'm serious. Keep quiet and listen to me." They reached the top of the stairs, and Lynn turned toward the end of the hall where Slocum had been staying. Duvall followed directly behind her like a ghost. "I'm gonna have a look around this room while you tell me everything you know about this man. I wanna know everything he said when he stepped into this place, everything he did while he was here, and anywhere he's been since."

She tried to keep her tears to herself, but Lynn's voice cracked as she relayed every little detail she could remember.

Even so, she refrained from describing any of the more intimate moments while Duvall rooted through Slocum's things.

"Did he ask about the reward?" he asked. When he didn't get a reply, Duvall stuck his pistol in Lynn's face and thumbed back the hammer.

"Yes," she said in a rush. "Everyone asks about it. Those damn notices are tacked up everywhere."

"Is that why he's here?"

"He's been more interested in the Chesterton Mining Company."

"Is that a fact?"

She nodded as if she was ashamed of herself, and then looked out the window. The sound of cracking wood drew her attention back to where Duvall was recklessly pulling out a drawer to toss it against the bed.

"Why the hell would he go to the Chesterton Mining Company?" he asked.

"I just rented his room, which I do for a living, so will you *stop* making such a mess?"

Duvall wheeled around to fix her with a venomous stare. He held his Smith & Wesson in one hand and the splintered remains of another drawer in the other. At the moment, it seemed just as likely that he would hit her with either object. "He was just here," Duvall pointed out.

"I don't know what you're—"

Snapping his hand toward her, Duvall sent the chunk of broken wood sailing past her left cheek. It was impossible to say whether it was a very precise throw or a near miss. "Someone was in this room lately and I don't wanna hear it was you!" he growled. "I track men for a living, and I've been tracking this one long enough to know he's not far away. I can smell him."

"If your nose is so good, then why are you asking me so many questions?"

"You're a real smart-mouthed bitch, ain't you?"

Lynn scowled back at him, but it was plain to see that she

was fearful of the stranger. Duvall pressed his advantage by taking a quick step closer and looming over her.

"He skinned out that window, didn't he?" Duvall asked.

Lynn glanced toward the window, but didn't say a word. The look on her face made it obvious she was thinking about something awfully hard, though.

"Yeah," Duvall said as he nodded. "I think he did. And since you're not saying so right away, that leads me to believe you've got a lot more to hide. Maybe I shouldn't take it so easy on you."

"I don't want any trouble in my house," she said. "That's all. Just because that mining company posts its notices everywhere doesn't mean this whole town is out for blood."

"Tell me whatever you were hiding before and there doesn't need to be any more blood spilled. At least, not your blood."

After a slight pause, Lynn said, "He did go through that window. He must have heard you were coming or something else spooked him."

"When will he be back?"

"I don't even know if he will come back."

Suddenly, Duvall's hand snapped out to clip her across the face. "Don't lie to me anymore! His things are still here. His horse is outside. He'll be back."

"I don't know when!" As Duvall cocked his hand as if he was notching an arrow, she winced and added, "Honestly. Hitting me won't change that."

"Where'd he go?"

"I don't know. He just went away. I came up to tend to your room and saw he was leaving. He hopped out the window and there wasn't anything I could do about it. He paid in advance, so what do I care? I just don't want any trouble in my place!"

"How long ago did he leave?"

"Right when you were coming back inside."

That was the truth and Duvall knew it. He made good on his promise to leave her alone, and stalked toward the window. "Which way was he headed when he left?"

"I don't know. You were coming inside, so I hurried downstairs to meet you. Surely, you remember back that far."

Duvall grumbled under his breath as he pulled the window open and stuck his head out. The street below was mostly empty, apart from a few shapes that wandered in between other houses and darkened storefronts. Something made a hissing sound to his left, so Duvall turned to see what it was. Instead of finding a bird or some other sort of animal, he saw Slocum crouched on the roof, hanging on to one of the eaves that jutted from the house's second floor. Slocum grabbed Duvall's collar with his free hand and yanked the man outside.

Lynn yelped in surprise when she saw Duvall get hauled, kicking and flailing, through the window. She ran to see what had happened, and was treated to the sight of Duvall being dangled by his shirt. "Were you there the whole time?" she asked Slocum.

"Yeah," Slocum grunted as he struggled to maintain his grip on both Duvall and the house. "Why do you think I insisted on you telling him everything he wanted to know?"

"I thought you just didn't want me to get into any trouble."

"Well, there's that, too. But," Slocum added as he shook Duvall and pulled him up a bit, "this asshole insisted on making trouble anyways. Didn't you?"

"You're the one that started the trouble," Duvall snarled. "Killing a man like Patrick Chesterton calls down all kinds of trouble."

"I've never even met Patrick Chesterton," Slocum told him. "But from what I've heard, there's a long line of folks who'd like to do him some harm."

"Say whatever you want. You killed him and there's a reward for your head. I found you, so I'm gonna collect it."

Slocum saw the gun in Duvall's hand. More importantly, he noticed that Duvall had gotten enough of his bearings to take aim and put that gun to work. Without the slightest bit of panic, Slocum pulled Duvall's collar in one direction and then sharply snapped him in another. "Collect your reward from down there," he said as he pitched Duvall toward the edge of the roof.

"Oh, my Lord!" Lynn yelped when she saw Duvall tumble.

The roof was angled in such a way that made it next to impossible for Duvall to break his momentum. It had been tough enough for Slocum to hang on and stay put using a handhold, but Duvall put up a good fight as he slipped along the weathered shingles. His feet bounced off the roof and his hands flapped uselessly while trying to find something to grab. Thanks to the way Slocum had thrown him, Duvall was rolling more or less on his side when he hit the edge. The thumping racket stopped for a second and was followed by a heavy thump.

"Is he . . . dead?" Lynn asked.

Slocum chuckled and hauled himself in through the window. "There's one way to find out."

He ran through his room, bolted down the stairs, and practically flew through the front door. His Colt Navy was in his grasp as he bounded off the porch and made his way to the spot where Duvall had landed. Sure enough, the other man was lying in a heap right where he should have been.

"You hung on to your gun," Slocum said as he bent down to snatch that gun away from its owner. "That's some mighty fine dedication in a bounty hunter."

"I'm a representative of . . . the law . . . and I intend to . . ."

Slocum ended that sentence by using his boot to roll Duvall onto his back. "An uppity bounty hunter, no less," he growled. "Which means you've got no redeeming qualities whatsoever. Did you break anything in your fall?"

Duvall curled into a ball and let out a strained grunt. Instead of reacting to the impact he'd just sustained, he stretched a hand toward a small holster strapped inside the top of his boot. Slocum's foot came down hard, pinning Duvall's elbow to the ground with his fingers less than an inch from drawing the holdout pistol.

"Looks like you've still got some fight in you," Slocum

said. "That means you're probably pretty healthy. Let's just put that to the test, shall we?"

Slocum kept his boot pressed against Duvall's elbow until he'd taken the little .32 from its ankle holster. From there, Slocum repositioned his stance so he could grab Duvall by the collar and lift him to his feet. Right about then, Lynn rushed outside and nervously took in the sight before her.

"You shouldn't move a man after he's fallen like that," she said. "What if something was broken?"

"He looks all right to me," Slocum said. The instant Duvall tried to move, Slocum shook him as if he was punishing a rag doll. "Aw, he looks just fine. How about I bring him in for some coffee? You like coffee, bounty hunter? Sure you do!"

Slocum shoved Duvall into the boardinghouse, and Lynn followed along behind them. She looked around at the neighboring buildings, and must have seen a few curious faces staring back at her. Either that, or she simply assumed folks were watching, because she shrugged and smiled nervously as if to calm a small audience.

Once inside, Slocum marched Duvall over to the closest chair and tossed him toward it. The bounty hunter stumbled a few steps before his legs hit the chair and he awkwardly fell onto the seat. Rather than get up or struggle, he adjusted to a proper sitting position as though he'd intended to take a load off his feet the entire time.

"What happened?" Lynn asked as she hurried inside and shut the door. "Who is this man? For that matter, who the hell are both of you?"

Slocum had already dropped Duvall's Smith & Wesson into his holster, so he tucked the smaller holdout pistol under his belt right beside it. Pointing his Colt Navy at the man in the chair, Slocum said, "The last time this one and I crossed paths, he was shooting at me from a distance. He also fired a few shots at some poor old miner."

"I didn't shoot any miner," Duvall grunted.

"Really? Then I suppose that was just some sort of delusion on my part."

"Isn't that what you want me to believe when it comes to you gunning down Patrick Chesterton?"

Slocum shrugged his shoulders and replied, "You might just have a point there."

Tired of being ignored, Lynn stormed over to a spot where both men could see her. "If I don't get some answers pretty damn quickly, I'll insist both of you get off my property!"

Shifting his eyes toward her without letting his gun waver from where it was aimed, Slocum asked, "Did he hurt you?"

Lynn blinked and fought to maintain her angry visage. "A little."

Slocum shook his head and stared at Duvall with a set of narrow, murderous eyes. "That wasn't such a good idea, mister."

Lynn moved forward to place a hand on Slocum's shoulder. "I'm fine, Adam. He just . . . wait a second. Is Adam really your name?"

Letting out a sigh, Slocum told her, "No. This asshole was right about one thing. I am John Slocum."

"Oh, my Lord," Lynn moaned.

"But I didn't kill Patrick Chesterton. That's why I came here. All of those notices are being circulated well past this town." Focusing on Duvall, he asked, "Where did you come from?"

Grudgingly, Duvall replied, "San Antonio."

"See?" Slocum said. "I told you. Hold on. San Antonio?"

Duvall nodded as a smug grin slid across his face.

"Shit," Slocum growled. "I was tossed in jail not far from here and about to be handed over to some hired gun on account of that damned notice. Now, I hear this has spread all the way down into Texas!"

"You were about to be handed over to me," Duvall said. "Sheriff White has steered me to plenty of good rewards in the Montana Territory."

"All for a slice of the profits without having to do more than his normal job?" Slocum grunted.

"That's right. And breaking out of jail won't help your case any. If anything, you'll only be worth more."

Lynn's eyes were wide as saucers as she placed her hands over her mouth and backed away from the two men. "You're John Slocum? You broke out of jail?"

"It ain't too late to get out of this mess, ma'am," Duvall told her. "Help me now and we can set everything straight again."

Lynn's eyes narrowed as she spoke to Duvall through gritted teeth. "You're all sweet talk and promises, but you were a lot different when you were threatening me and slapping my face."

"She's got you there," Slocum said. When her angry gaze was turned in his direction, he quickly bit his tongue.

"And *you*!" Lynn said. "After we . . . after all you said when . . . I'm not even sure what to think of you."

"He's a killer," Duvall said. "Plain and simple."

"He's also the one who stopped you from doing anything else to me," Lynn pointed out. "And he's *not* the one who raised his hand against a defenseless woman just to get what he wanted."

Duvall scowled and turned away from her as if Lynn had simply stopped existing. "Sounds to me like he already got what he wanted."

Lynn's hand flashed out so quickly that Slocum didn't have a chance to stop her from slapping the bounty hunter. Of course, even if he'd known what she was going to do a week or two ahead of time, he still wouldn't have stopped her. The blow landed with more sound than fury, but was still enough to rattle Duvall's back teeth.

"That's for striking me," she snapped. Holding up that same hand to Slocum, she added, "And I won't have any more violence committed in my house. Do you understand me?"

"Yes," Slocum said with a polite nod. "Do you think it's possible for us to have some coffee?"

Taken slightly aback by the request, Lynn said, "I suppose so. I could use a drink of something to calm my nerves."

After watching Lynn leave the room, Slocum lunged toward Duvall and jammed the barrel of his Colt under the bounty hunter's chin. "Make one move or one sound without my permission and I'll decorate these pretty walls with your brains. Understand?"

Duvall nodded as best he could under the circumstances.

"I didn't harm a hair on Patrick Chesterton's head. Someone has taken it upon themselves to spread the word that I have and that's got to stop. You're gonna help make that happen."

"Why?" Duvall croaked. "You'll kill me either way."

"Why would I go through all this trouble just to kill you later?"

Duvall pondered that quietly, but Slocum could tell there were plenty of wheels beginning to turn within the bounty hunter's mind.

"You're so good at finding men that don't want to be found, I want you to help me deal with Patrick Chesterton," Slocum said.

"He's dead."

"Then we'll track down a body. If he was murdered, I'd be more than happy to help you find the asshole that did it. If he's alive and kicking, then there are plenty of folks around town who'd be interested to hear that as well. Patrick owed a lot of men a lot of money, and I've already arranged for a finder's fee if we make Patrick answer for those debts. Do you know who Patrick's family is?"

"Of course."

"Then you must know how grateful they would be if we discovered Patrick was still alive. If he's dead, I'll help you find the killer and split the reward money with you."

"Split it? I didn't come all this way to split that reward."

"You also didn't come all this way to be dragged out of a boardinghouse, gutted, and dumped into a shallow hole," Slocum snarled. "But those are your two choices."

Just then, Lynn walked into the room. "Would you men like sugar in your coffee?"

"Yes," Slocum replied cheerfully. "That would be fine."

14

The three of them had their coffee, and even ate some stale cookies that Lynn had baked a few days before. If not for the fact that one man had thrown the other off the roof of the house, it would have seemed like a very civilized affair. There wasn't a lot of talking, but it did Lynn some good to see things were under control. No matter how calm she was, however, she didn't forget about the circumstances that had brought them all together.

"I don't want him in this house," she whispered to Slocum as she gathered up the cups.

Duvall sat in a chair, sipping coffee and staring out a window.

"I don't intend on keeping him here," Slocum said. "I just want to lay low for a little while to make sure nobody saw what happened."

"One of the neighbors had to see something, but I doubt they'll say anything."

"Really? Why?"

"Because two of them are elderly and too afraid to answer their door. The rest would rather die before going to any of those Chesterton guards for help. Not that those brutes would do anything anyway unless they knew the whole story."

"Well, if this bounty hunter had any partners, they would have come to bust him out of here by now."

Suddenly, Lynn's eyes widened. "You mean you thought more gunmen might come here?"

"If there were others, they would have come and questioned you once I left anyhow," Slocum replied. "And I doubt they'd be as gentle as this one was. I wanted to make sure I was here if anyone else showed up. No, there aren't any others. I'm sure of it now."

After steeling herself with a deep breath, she asked, "Are you really John Slocum?"

He nodded. "Sorry to lie before, but it's not exactly safe to say my name too loudly in this town."

"Did you kill Patrick Chesterton?"

"If I had, would I come right back here to confront anyone at Chesterton Mining?" When he didn't get a response from Lynn, he placed a finger under her chin and lifted her face so she was looking at him when he said, "No. I wouldn't. I came here to put an end to this so that reward can be taken off the table. I've got enough men coming after me as it is without another incentive like that."

"Why would men be coming after you?"

"That's a real long story. Maybe I'll tell some of it to you once this is done. For now, how about I take this bounty hunter out of your sight?"

"And do what with him?"

Brushing his hand against the cheek that had been slapped, Slocum asked, "Any suggestions?"

"Just see to it that he doesn't come back. Wait! I didn't mean that you should—"

"I know what you meant. Since I'll be going along with him, there won't be a reason for him to come here again."

"Where are you going?"

"I already told you that," Slocum replied.

"But won't he just try to hurt you again?"

"If he does, I can handle him. I've handled plenty of bounty hunters in my day. This one's different."

"How so?"

With a gleam in his eye, Slocum told her, "He's after the same thing I am."

"So you're telling me that his own men told you that Patrick Chesterton is still alive?"

Slocum nodded at Duvall and handed over the bounty hunter's pistol. "Yep."

Both men walked down a wide street that was lined on both sides by livery stables and merchants that sold everything from saddles to riding crops. Since most folks weren't interested in shopping for their riding needs at this time of night, those shops were dark. A few of the stables had a single worker minding the place, but they weren't interested in two men passing by on foot.

Duvall took his gun back, idly checked the cylinder, and wasn't too surprised by what he'd found.

"It ain't loaded," Slocum confirmed. "And I ain't stupid."

"You are if you think I have any interest in helping you."

"Whatever Patrick's friends or enemies are saying, Isabelle Chesterton believes he's dead. I only had to meet her once to gather that much."

"Then she won't have any problem in making good on the reward for your head. What the hell do I care if Patrick is alive or dead?"

"Because there's a hell of a lot more to be made by digging down to the truth."

Duvall stopped in his tracks. Hearing the voices of some drunks in a nearby saloon, he walked to a spot on the boardwalk that was thick with shadows and beyond the reach of the nearest torch posted along the side of the street. "How do you figure?" he asked.

Knowing he had the man hooked, Slocum followed the bounty hunter while keeping his hand resting on the grip of his Colt. "If Patrick is playing dead, there's bound to be a good reason for it. Since his family runs one of the biggest mining operations in this territory, that reason's bound to have something to do with money."

"Could be he just wants to get away from his family."

"If that's the case, don't you think you'll at least get your money if you're the one to break the good news to the rest of the Chestertons?"

"Turning you in would be a lot easier," Duvall pointed out. "Less mucking around in a rich family's bullshit."

Slocum nodded, dug a few bullets from his pocket, and tossed them at Duvall's feet. "You think taking me in will be easier? There's your ammunition. Load your gun and go to work. I'd prefer to settle this face-to-face anyhow."

Duvall held Slocum's stare better than most men. The bounty hunter had enough sand to keep from backing down, but he also had enough sense to keep from making a move to reload his gun.

"You say you'd split the reward?" Duvall asked.

Feeling the hook sink in a little deeper, Slocum added, "But I also intend on soaking Isabelle Chesterton for more than fifteen thousand dollars. You're just doing your job and I can respect that. I have a bigger bone to pick with the ones that printed those notices and drug my name through the dirt for no good reason. My single meeting with her also told me she doesn't care to waste her time with anything that ain't involved with her company. She needs to be taught how much damage can be done when being so careless about things like this.

"I came all this way to put an end to it, but I'll also make it worth my while. I don't need your help, but it would be appreciated. If you see this through, it'll be worth your while, too."

Scowling, Duvall asked, "You're willing to trust me as a partner?"

"Trust you? Hell, no. I'm willing to work with a bounty hunter because it could make this a little easier. The only thing I trust about you is that you'll know my offer is the smartest way for you to come out of this alive and with some cash in your pocket."

"Sure. If we could keep things civil for however long it'll take to see this through, everything would be just fine."

Slocum patted the bounty hunter's shoulder and told him, "It's not gonna take half as long as you might think."

The Chesterton Mining Company was even darker on this night than it was when Slocum had taken a gander at it the previous night. After biding their time for a while, he and Duvall walked right up to the building as if they intended on walking straight in to apply for mineral rights to a new patch of land. Not one window had a light behind it, leaving the place looking more like a shell than a prosperous business.

"You said you were going to meet someone here?" Duvall asked.

Slocum nodded confidently. "That's right. They're supposed to keep an eye out for me tonight."

"And you really think they did?"

Rather than answer that question, Slocum nodded in the direction of a small livery built to keep the horses of employees or of visitors to the mining company. Several figures lurked in the shadows over there, slowly working their way toward the broad doorway like rats sniffing cautiously at a hunk of cheese.

Tad was the first to step forward enough to be seen in the dim glow of moonlight. "You didn't say you'd come with anyone."

"Too bad," Slocum replied. "Where's Trick?"

"Close. You wanna talk here?"

"No. There's a stable at the end of this road on the eastern corner."

Tad nodded. "I know the one."

"Meet us there in half an hour," Slocum said. "If you're late, I'll see to it that all the wrong people find out about Trick's current state of good health."

Without saying anything, Tad backed into the shadows to

converse with the rest of the rats. Although the decision wasn't popular among the rodents, they agreed and dispersed.

Once it was clear that others were gone, Duvall asked, "What the hell was that all about?"

"Just seeing this thing through. I thought you'd be happy that we're already so far along."

Both men walked away from the mining company, but Slocum quickly led Duvall in a different direction than the one he'd mentioned to Tad. "You'll just be going into an ambush if you go to that meeting," Duvall said.

"Yeah, but Patrick will be there."

"How can you be so sure?"

"He's got to get a look at us for himself," Slocum replied. "After all the trouble he went through to concoct a fake death, he'll want to see what we know or how big of a threat we are to his plans. Having you along when he was only expecting me will just stir him up that much more."

"I suppose you got something else to go by other than your gut?"

"Nope."

Duvall stopped, looked around suspiciously, and put his back to the nearest wall. "This is crazy. You're walking into what's bound to be a trap, knowing damn well you'll be outgunned, just on a hunch that you'll make it out alive?"

"I've got more than a hunch I'll make it out alive," Slocum replied. "Those assholes already took a shot at me, and they barely kept from shooting themselves in their feet. Besides, if this is a trap, don't you think you can sniff it out before we get there?"

"Probably."

"Then that's how you'll earn your part of this reward money. And before you think of double-crossing me, those men will want to kill anyone who knows about Trick. That includes me and you."

"That could change when they find out who you are," Duvall pointed out.

"They don't know John Slocum's face from Adam Clay's. Even a half-wit would just shoot us both to be safe."

After thinking it over, Duvall sighed. "Are you gonna let me load my weapon?"

Slocum grinned. "A big, bad bounty hunter like yourself can make do without a pistol, can't he?"

Knowing it wouldn't do any good to argue the point, Duvall kept walking.

Even after circling around to approach the stable from an angle that would allow them to see the structure as well as the street it faced, Slocum and Duvall arrived well ahead of schedule. Slocum picked out a few figures lurking in the darkness surrounding the wide, barnlike building. One man stood at a side doorway, holding a lantern.

"There's your ambush," Duvall said.

"Right. Now let's see what else we can find."

Every step of the way, Slocum waited for the bounty hunter to bolt from him. He kept Duvall in his sight, and still managed to watch the stable for any suspicious movement. Sneaking around the back of the stable, Slocum kept his head down, and only walked when the rustling wind could cover the sound of his steps. The bounty hunter didn't need to be prompted to follow suit.

After spotting a rifleman hiding in the stable's loft, Slocum hunkered down and squinted at a cluster of three men. Then, he felt a tap on his shoulder.

"If Patrick's here, he'll be right there," Duvall said after catching Slocum's attention. "I'd put my money on the short fella with the big hat. He's standing close to those other two like he wished he was glued to 'em."

Slocum nodded. "Have you ever seen Patrick Chesterton?"

"No, but that short one's gotta be him. Look at the cut of those clothes. They're not something bought off a pile like the rags those other boys are wearing. And by the way he's fidgeting, he looks like he's the one that wants to be here the least."

Now that his eyes had adjusted to the shadows, Slocum could see what Duvall was talking about. He didn't recognize expensive stitching or fine thread, but he could make out a difference in the way the shortest of those three other men was dressed. What had caught Slocum's eye was the gun around the short fellow's waist. It was a pearl-handled .38 that was most definitely worth a pretty penny. Also, the leather of the holster barely looked worn in. Those things were enough to convince Slocum he was looking at a man who hired other men to protect him while wearing a pistol to make himself look tough. From what Slocum had gathered while being in town, that suited Trick Chesterton right down to the bone.

"All right," Slocum whispered. "You move around and approach that one with the lantern. He's obviously the one that's meant to catch our eye."

"Why should I go? You're the one they're waiting for."

"Why should I be the one to let you cover my back? Last time you saw my back when you had a gun in your hand, you tried to put a bullet into it. Besides, I made my offer rather than put you down, so now it's time for you to show you're worth the effort."

"And how do I know you won't just shoot me?" Duvall asked.

"Because it would have been a whole lot easier for me to do that much a long time ago. Now get in there and do some fast talking. All you need to do is make certain Patrick Chesterton is alive. Anything goes wrong, and I'll cover you."

Duvall shook his head and sighed. If he had more objections to the situation, he didn't bother voicing them. He did, however, move away from Slocum to circle around and slip through some more shadows before stepping into the street and walking toward the man with the lantern.

Slocum didn't trust bounty hunters farther than he could toss them and their horses. But if there was one thing he had faith in, it was that bounty hunters would go wherever the money was. That was their biggest fault as well as their biggest asset. At the very least, this particular bounty hunter was good for drawing some fire if Trick's men intended on blasting the first warm body they laid eyes on.

After moving to another spot where he could watch as much of the stable as possible, Slocum drew his pistol and kept it ready. He then kept his eyes trained on the stable so he could get used to every flicker of the lantern and each black pool of shadow. Before long, the men waiting there stuck out like they all held lanterns, and the rifleman hiding in the loft might as well have been standing up and waving at him.

Duvall got closer than Slocum had expected before the men at the stable reacted. The cluster of three huddled just inside the main doorway as the man with the lantern strode forward. Once the lantern carrier got a bit closer, Slocum could see the familiar scar running down the guard's chin and neck.

"That's close enough," Scar said. "Where the hell is the other one?"

"He's close enough to pick off any one of you men that decide to try and take a shot at me," Duvall said. "Where's Patrick?"

"Who the hell wants to know?"

"My name's Duvall. If Patrick is here, it'd be best for him to step forward sooner rather than later. I've got a proposition he'll want to hear."

"What sort of proposition would you have for a dead man?" Scar asked.

"It's about the family business. That mining company is about to run into some tough times real damn quickly. Of course, if he is dead, then he won't mind if that company goes belly up. It'd be like one big tombstone to mark his passing."

Before those words were fully out of Duvall's mouth, the little fellow stepped forward. At first, it looked as if he meant to push aside his two companions in his haste to get closer to Duvall. Then, Slocum could tell the fellow had grabbed onto the other men's sleeves and was dragging them along.

Slocum chuckled under his breath and shook his head at the sight.

Practically throwing Tad and another stocky fellow in front of him, the little man in the big hat snapped, "What the hell do you know about my mining company?"

Now that the little man was closer to Duvall, Slocum could get a better sense as to his real size. The fellow wasn't quite as small as he'd first appeared, simply because the men guarding him were so big. The hat he wore, on the other hand, was undeniably several sizes too large for him.

"Patrick Chesterton?" Duvall asked.

The smaller fellow propped his hands on his hips and replied, "I'm a Chesterton. What difference does it make which one I am?"

"You're right. Maybe I'll just come back to the mining company during proper business hours and discuss it then."

"I'm Patrick Chesterton," the little man sputtered. "What do you have to say about my business?"

"How do I know you're really Patrick?"

The smaller man sighed. "You're the one that insisted I show up."

"No, he ain't, Pat," Tad said. "It was the other one we was telling you about."

"Oh, for Christ's sake!"

"Fine," Duvall said. "I suppose I'll believe you."

"Great. What do you have to say about my mining company?"

"It may not be your company for much longer," the bounty hunter said. "In fact, before too much longer, it won't belong to anyone that goes by the name of Chesterton."

All of the men tensed like bowstrings, but Patrick seemed ready to snap. Both of his fists clenched and he spoke through tightly gritted teeth. "What do you mean by that? Tell me right now, goddammit. Is it something my sister did? It is, isn't it? What did she do? *Tell me!*"

It wasn't until that very moment that Slocum was certain he was looking at Patrick Chesterton. Only someone with a vested interest in the subject matter would get so supremely bent out of shape by what Duvall had said. And only a Chesterton would be ready to draw blood when someone got close to sullying the family livelihood.

Duvall must have sensed he'd struck pay dirt as well, because he took a reflexive step back and moved his hand toward his gun.

"All right," Slocum said to himself. "Here we go."

15

As Patrick Chesterton stomped forward, the men on either side of him fanned out. Even Scar stepped away from the stable, carrying his lantern in one hand and a pistol in the other.

"You wanted to talk about my mining company, so talk," Patrick snarled as he bared his teeth like a rabid little dog.

Duvall backed up a few steps before deciding that wasn't going to help him any. "If I'd wanted to fight, I would have dropped all of your men already. We can have a discussion like men or you can all die like animals."

Patrick and his four guards lined up in front of Duvall. Although most of them had their weapons drawn, they didn't seem prepared to use them. Patrick, on the other hand, looked ready to draw blood using his bare hands. "You'd better finish what you were saying before, or I'll get impatient."

Sighting along the barrel of his pistol, Duvall said, "Keep flapping your gums, little man, and you won't have to pretend to be dead."

Feeling the tension crackle through the air, the men guarding Patrick moved forward. In particular, Scar walked toward the bounty hunter with his lantern held in front of him. "You think you can take us all?" he asked.

Without hesitation, Duvall nodded. "With time to spare."

The certainty in his eyes was enough to put Tad and his partner in check. Scar, however, continued to inch forward.

"Who the hell do you think you are? Did that bitch Isabelle hire you?" Scar asked.

"Hey!" Patrick snapped. "Only I can talk about my sister like that!"

"Don't take another step," Duvall warned.

Scar squinted and stretched his neck to get a closer look at the bounty hunter. When he also stretched out the hand holding the lantern, he almost got close enough to knock it against the barrel of Duvall's gun. Suddenly, the ugly guard smirked. "That gun of yers ain't even loaded."

"What?" Patrick asked.

Nodding even as Duvall tried to pull his gun out of the lantern's direct light, Scar said, "I can see from here. There ain't no glint off'a no bullets in the cylinder."

"I wouldn't test him if I were you," Slocum said as he stepped up to stand beside the bounty hunter. "There's a hell of a lot to lose if you're mistaken."

"Finally," Patrick said as he settled in behind the biggest of his guards. "You're the one that had something to say to me."

"Why, yes, I am."

"Who might you be?"

Planting his feet and steeling every nerve in his body until all of his muscles were drawn taut, Slocum replied, "I'm John Slocum. And if you didn't think all those notices would catch my attention, you're even dumber than you look in that oversized hat."

Patrick Chesterton froze.

All of the guards straightened up and looked to their employer for a hint as to what they should do.

The rifleman in the loft raised his weapon to his shoulder.

Duvall let out a strained breath, obviously wishing he had a bullet or two for his pistol.

"You can't be John Slocum," Patrick said. "You're supposed to be in a jail down in Mexico."

"Is that why you tossed my name about like that? You should get your facts straight before you put a price on a man's head."

"I didn't put out that reward," Patrick whined. "It was Isabelle."

"Yeah, but whose idea was it to pin your death on me?" Slocum asked. When he didn't get anything but silence in response to the question, he nodded and growled, "That's what I thought. Well, your mistake is gonna cost you."

Assuming the cost was something he didn't want to pay, Patrick yelped, "Kill him!"

Slocum already had his target in mind, and immediately shifted his aim up toward the loft where the rifleman was looking down on everyone else. His first shot felt rushed, so he sent another right after it. The Colt barked in Slocum's hand, illuminating his face in the flash of exploding gunpowder. The rifleman fired a shot, which hissed well above Slocum's head. Once the figure in the loft fell backward, Slocum shifted his attention to the rest of his problems.

In the two seconds that had passed since Patrick's command, the guards closed ranks. The stocky man next to Tad fired a quick shot, but was too panicked to hit anything. Tad might have done something if Patrick wasn't jostling him so much in his desperate attempt to get behind him for cover. The more Patrick tried to get behind Tad, the more Tad turned to see what the hell the smaller fellow was doing, resulting in a dance that was similar to a big dog chasing its tail.

Duvall might not have a loaded gun, but he did have a shoulder and plenty of muscle to put behind it. The bounty hunter charged Scar, slammed his shoulder into his gut, and doubled him over. The gun in Scar's hand went off, but sent its round into the earth with a sharp thump.

Not wanting to risk hitting Duvall, Slocum shifted his aim back to the larger group of men. The stocky bodyguard stood with his arm extended to steady his aim. Slocum dropped to his knee a split second before the stocky man pulled his trigger. Hot lead whipped a few inches over Slocum's hat as he returned fire. The shot hit the stocky man in the torso and forced him back a step, but the shot right after it blazed a hole through the guard's skull. The stocky man's arms drooped from his shoulders as he wobbled upon his feet. Then, he dropped to both knees and fell over dead.

Another shot was fired so close to Slocum that it caused him to hop back and wheel around toward its source. Scar had been the one to pull his trigger, and Slocum had to thank Duvall for keeping the guard too busy to shoot straight. The bounty hunter tussled with Scar, using one hand to grip the wrist of the guard's gun hand and the other hand to clench Scar's throat.

"Son of a . . . bitch!" Scar grunted as he struggled to pull his gun arm loose. Since that was a lost cause, he used his free hand to try and cave in Duvall's head with the lantern.

Duvall tilted his head to one side to avoid the lantern, but it still thumped against his shoulder and the side of his neck hard enough to rattle his eyeballs. Duvall brought his knee up to pound against Scar's midsection, which caused the guard to press his neck even harder against Duvall's hand. When Duvall tightened his grip, Scar's eyes nearly bulged from their sockets.

Slocum was about to lend a hand with Duvall's situation, but realized his help wasn't exactly needed. Once the bounty hunter had twisted Scar's wrist to force him to drop his gun, the odds were drastically evened. In fact, Duvall seemed to have the advantage since he was now able to slam his knees repeatedly against Scar's gut and balls while strangling the poor bastard with one hand.

Tracking the sound of scurrying footsteps, Slocum found Patrick making a run for the stables. He would have fired a warning shot, but didn't want to waste the ammo. Instead, he ran to catch up with the little man. On his way, Slocum was quickly reintroduced to Trick's second guard.

Tad had been checking on his fallen partner. It hadn't taken long for him to see the stocky man was beyond anyone's help, and just as Slocum was about to run by, Tad reached out to snag one of Slocum's legs.

Slocum's momentum carried him forward, but his right leg might as well have been rooted in solid rock. Thankfully, his other leg was stretched ahead to catch and hold his weight before he was forced to swallow a mouthful of dirt. Slocum twisted around and swung his pistol at Tad's wide, doughy face. The side of the Colt slapped against Tad's face like a wet rag. Even though the iron opened a nasty gash on the side of his head, Tad barely seemed to notice it. His eyes narrowed into angry slits and he let out his breath in a rumbling growl.

Slocum tried to pull his leg free, but couldn't. He cocked his arm back to fire a round at point-blank range, but lost his Colt completely when Tad slapped his gun hand with a strong, pawlike fist. While the Colt was still tumbling through the air, Slocum balled up his fist and drove it into Tad's chin. Judging by the subtle twitch in the bigger man's face, he felt less pain from receiving the punch than Slocum felt in delivering it. For a second, Slocum swore he'd broken a knuckle.

When Tad dropped his fist on Slocum's shoulder, the impact turned Slocum's knees to jelly and dropped him straight down. Before he could get back up, Slocum felt Tad's leg pound into him like a tree trunk swung by a giant from a fairy tale. Slocum fell backward and landed heavily on his shoulder blades. He stayed there for a second or two, struggling to pull a breath into lungs which had just been emptied. Blinking a few times, Slocum couldn't quite decide if he was looking up at a dark sky or if the powerful blow had somehow blinded him. Before he could reach a decision on the matter, he was picked up and hauled more or less to his feet.

"Shouldn't have come here," Tad said as he drove a fist into Slocum's midsection. Shaking him, he added, "Should've stayed in Mexico."

Slocum grabbed Tad's wrist and tried to break the big man's grip. When he couldn't make a dent there, he did his best to pull that hand away from his throat so he could at least draw a full breath. The trickle of air he bought himself felt like a gush of cool, refreshing water. He alternated kicking Tad with his left and right boots, neither of which did anything more than bounce off the big fellow.

"Now you got to die," Tad said.

A shot was fired from above. Slocum might have been out of sorts, but he recognized the sound of a rifle when he heard it. That sound also told him that the man in the loft wasn't as dead as he'd hoped. Having that extra bit of firepower on higher ground tipped the scales too far in Patrick's favor, which prompted Slocum to launch a few more desperate attacks.

Tightening his grip on Tad's wrist, Slocum drew both knees up toward his chest and then lashed out with one powerful kick. Both boot heels pounded against Tad's gut and forced a pained grunt from the big man's throat. Slocum pulled his legs up again and sent his next kick into Tad's knee. He heard a wet crunch and could feel something give within the bigger man's leg. A scowl crossed Tad's face, moments before he staggered back and crumpled.

The instant Tad's grip loosened, Slocum pulled free and took the man's pistol away from him. He wasted no time before jamming it into Tad's gut and pulling the trigger. The gun went off with a muffled thump, sending the big man back as if he'd been kicked by a mule. When he tried to put his weight on the leg with the broken knee, Tad fell and rolled onto his side.

Suddenly, the sound of wet meat sizzling on a griddle drifted through the air. That was followed by a pained scream and the shattering of glass. Slocum turned to find Duvall standing over Scar with a broken lantern in his hand. Judging by the way Scar reeled and held on to his bleeding cheek, it wasn't difficult to figure out how that lantern had been broken. If there was any doubt, the smell of spilled kerosene and the little flames sputtering on Scar's jacket painted a very clear picture.

Scar might have been in pain and starting to burn, but he had enough of his wits about him to lift his pistol and aim at Duvall.

"Watch it," Slocum barked as he tossed Tad's six-shooter.

Duvall snatched the pistol from the air, slipped his finger under the trigger guard, and fired before Scar could find his target. The bullet drilled through Scar's forehead, snapped his head back, and launched a spray of pulpy brain matter from the back of the guard's skull.

"You all right?" Slocum asked.

Duvall took a moment to let the pistol he'd been given settle within his grasp. Shifting his eyes to Slocum, he replied, "A little bruised, but I should survive. What about the big fellows?"

"One's dead and the other," Slocum said as he glanced over to Tad, "looks like he won't be going anywhere."

Tad rolled on the ground, clasping his broken knee with both hands and bleeding from a gaping wound in his side. If he carried any other weapons, the pain from his wounds made him forget about them completely.

"Patrick's around here somewhere," Duvall said.

Slocum rushed over to Tad, just to be certain the big man was unarmed. All he could find was a knife strapped to Tad's boot, and he was able to take that away without a fuss. "That little prick's probably run to the hills by now."

"No," Duvall said sternly. "He'll stick close to any men he's got left. My money's on that stable. Isn't there a rifleman still up in that loft?"

"Yeah. He's also stopped shooting. I thought he was dead."

Gripping his pistol, Duvall said, "One way to find out." With that, the bounty hunter ran toward the stable.

Since Duvall was going in through the side door Scar had been guarding earlier, Slocum crept toward the main entrance. By the time he reached the wide double doors,

Slocum had reloaded his pistol and was ready for war. Unfortunately, he wasn't ready for the ax handle that was swung at him from the shadows just inside those doors. Slocum caught the thick piece of timber squarely in the stomach and was dropped to one knee.

"Mackie!" Patrick shouted. "Down here by the main doors!"

The blow to the stomach hurt, but Slocum had managed to tense a portion of his muscles on impact. He gritted his teeth through the pain and fought the urge to lunge at the smaller man. Just as he'd hoped, Slocum didn't have to wait more than a second or two before Patrick tried to press his advantage. When Patrick swung the ax handle again, Slocum stepped in, turned to take the hit on his ribs, and then dropped his arm down to trap the makeshift weapon.

Patrick had been grinning right until he realized he could no longer reclaim his ax handle. Rather than try to test his strength against Slocum's hold, he let the handle go and turned to run farther into the stables. Slocum rushed after him, but was stopped by the distinctive sound of a rifle's lever being ratcheted back and forth. Skidding on the straw-covered floor, Slocum was just able to change directions before the man in the loft fired down at him. Mackie's bullet punched a hole into the floor in the spot where Slocum would have been if he'd continued along a straight line.

Slocum swung his pistol toward the loft and fired a few quick rounds. It was so dark up there that he couldn't be certain whether he was aiming at Mackie or a bale of hay. Hoping he'd at least forced the rifleman to move, Slocum got his legs beneath him and continued chasing Patrick.

Scampering footsteps sounded throughout the lower portion of the stables, followed by the nervous shuffle of the single horse being kept there for the night. Slocum could only make out a vague figure rushing through the dark, but he didn't have any trouble seeing the dim light from outside once Patrick shoved open another side door and bolted through it.

Slocum ran across the middle of the stables, which was mostly open territory. The moment he heard movement directly above him, he knew the rifleman was drawing a bead on him from the loft. Less than a second after that, a barrage of gunfire erupted from behind Slocum's position. He turned to see the last few shots exploding from Duvall's pistol to blast through the bottom of the loft. After that, came the definitive thump of deadweight followed by the rifle toppling all the way down to the floor.

"Go after him," Duvall said. "I'll circle around to cut him off."

With precious little time to waste, Slocum took the bounty hunter's suggestion.

16

The stretch of road that Patrick used was mostly dark and empty. So far, the only ones to check on all the gunshots were a few curious transients who kept mostly to the alleys and ditches alongside the street. A few locals peeked out from some windows, which was all Slocum could see as he ran after the living dead man. From what Lynn had told him, the Chesterton guards would have been the ones to investigate the disturbance anyhow.

As he ran, Patrick seemed almost as concerned with keeping his hat on his head as he was with outpacing his pursuers. With one hand pressed tightly against the oversized Stetson, he stretched his other hand backward to fire a series of wild shots in Slocum's general direction. All he managed to hit was a few walls, a window, and one very unlucky mule. Even after he'd fired off his last bullet, Patrick continued pulling his trigger.

Slocum pumped his legs as fast as he could to catch up to the slippery little cuss. When he'd heard the gunshots, he'd veered to run behind some posts for whatever cover they might provide. He'd slowed a bit to keep from presenting too big a target, and then had continued running in

161

earnest after he heard the slap of a hammer against spent bullet casings.

More than once, Slocum nearly lost sight of Patrick. The man might have been able to duck behind something or slip away completely, if not for the ridiculous hat he insisted on protecting with his life. Slocum forced some more steam into his legs, and tore down an alley that was so dark it could have been hiding an elephant. Slocum gambled that Patrick wasn't leading him into another ambush. Trick moved less like a man with a plan, and more like a card cheat who'd been caught with five aces in his hand.

Slocum's breaths became haggard and scratched his throat. His legs burned and all the parts of him that had recently been punched or kicked flared with sharp pains. Just as he was about to slow down, he realized Patrick was headed toward Lynn's boardinghouse. Even if Trick didn't intend on paying Lynn a visit, Slocum wasn't about to take that chance. Feeling one last burst of energy, he ran with everything he had and practically flew at Patrick.

Several yards ahead, Trick took a quick glance over his shoulder. He let out a startled yelp when he spotted Slocum, but didn't make a sound before running into Duvall. Patrick simply hadn't seen the bounty hunter coming at him from the left, and hit Duvall with enough force to knock both men off their feet.

Slocum caught up to them in a matter of seconds, but had to skid to a halt before running them over. Instead of sacrificing his balance, Slocum leaned forward to drive his weight into Patrick and slam him even harder into the dirt. When Patrick could see straight again, he was looking down the barrel of Slocum's Colt Navy.

Duvall stepped up beside the fallen Chesterton. Slocum knew the bounty hunter had a gun. Now, all that remained was to see how he would use it. "Does he have any more weapons, Slocum?" Duvall asked.

"Why don't you check him?"

"Fine. Make sure he doesn't try anything." With that, Duvall patted every one of Trick's pockets and any other place where a gun or knife could be stored. When he was finished, he stood up and said, "Seems clean to me."

Slocum cursed himself inside for allowing Duvall to do the searching. At the time, he'd thought it would present the bounty hunter with a good opportunity to show his true colors. If Duvall made a move against him, Slocum would be ready to counter it. Now, Slocum had to wonder if Trick really had been searched properly. Slocum could go through the motions himself, but that would only present his back to the bounty hunter. He thought about all the times in the last few minutes when Duvall had had a good, clear shot at him. If the bounty hunter hadn't proven himself by now, he never would. Besides, Slocum knew all too well that damn near any man could turn on another at any time. Waiting around for that bolt of lightning to hit wouldn't make it strike any sooner.

Every one of Trick's breaths was becoming stronger than the one before. His disoriented wriggling was quickly growing into squirms that could build into another flailing escape attempt. Slocum put a stop to that by pinning him down using one knee on Trick's chest. Now, Patrick struggled like a worm on a hook.

"All right," Slocum said as he gripped Trick's face and forced him to look straight down the Colt's barrel. "Enough running for one night. Your men are all dead or close to it."

"Not all of 'em," Trick said.

"You may have a goddamn army at your command, but there ain't nobody around to help you right now."

That sunk in very quickly, and did a real nice job of wiping away the grin that was beginning to show on Trick's face.

"What the hell is the reason behind all of this anyhow?" Slocum asked. "Why'd you pretend to be dead?"

"It's complicated."

"Really? You think I'm too stupid to know what's going on? Is that why you plastered my name all over those reward notices?"

"I didn't print those notices!" Trick snapped. "That was my sister's doing."

"And was she also the one who decided to blame me for killing you?"

Raising his eyebrows, Trick grumbled, "I suppose that was my doing. But you were supposed to be in Mexico! What the hell are you doing in the Dakota Territory?"

"You know something?" Slocum mused. "I don't know whether I should be riled up by that cocky tone in your voice or admire you for having the stones to ask me that question."

"I needed to lay low for a while," Trick explained. "Really low. You ain't from around here, but trust me when I tell you my family is pretty well known in these parts."

For once, Slocum knew the little man wasn't just blowing his own horn. "Go on."

"I arranged to turn up missing, but I couldn't afford to have anyone come looking for me. It was easier all around if everyone thought I was dead. At least, for right now. Rather than set up someone around here, I took advantage of your . . . let's just say . . . your rather colorful reputation."

"Colorful reputation, huh?"

Trick nodded as best he could with Slocum's hand gripping his chin. "I've heard it told that you shot upwards of two dozen men over the course of one year! Some say more, some say less, but you're the closest thing to the devil according to some folks."

"You heard these things at saloons?" Slocum asked.

"More or less."

"Bullshit spouted by drunks."

"I've heard some of that same bullshit," Duvall said.

Instantly grabbing on to the rope he'd been thrown, Trick said, "There! You see?"

"Yeah, yeah," Slocum grunted. "I still don't see why I get to be blamed for a killing that never even happened."

"It was just supposed to be another story tacked on to all the other ones floating around out there," Trick said. "Not everyone knows who you are, but if they asked around long enough, something or other would crop up. More than likely, whatever story someone heard would make them too scared to come after you. Hell, most anyone in this town would probably be willing to write me off and move on. Even if they did decide to take it serious, I didn't think no harm would be done since—"

"Since I was supposed to be in Mexico," Slocum finished.

"Right!"

Slocum took a moment to think about where the hell Trick had gotten the idea that he was supposed to be in Mexico. He couldn't come up with anything right away, but that wasn't too surprising. Over the years, Slocum had heard wild rumors placing him anywhere from the Canadian wilderness to South American jungles. When drunks got to talking, there was no limit as to what they might come up with. Besides, some of those rumors were true.

"So what about the reward?" Duvall asked.

Trick looked over at him and said, "That was my sister's doing."

"Are you sure about that?"

"Yeah. I got friends in the Chesterton Mining Company and they all know for a fact it was her that posted that reward. Everyone in town knows it. Just ask around if you don't believe me."

"You are a Chesterton," Slocum pointed out. "I'd think you would have more than a few friends in that mining company."

"I got family and employees," Trick explained. "At least, I used to. Most of them have to think I'm dead. That's the whole point."

Sensing he was finally getting close to the very thing he'd been after, Slocum asked, "And what point is that exactly?"

Trick started to speak, but cut himself short. Clenching his lips together, he flicked his eyes back and forth between Slocum and Duvall. When Slocum pressed his gun barrel against Trick's head, the little man's eyes stopped waggling and fixed solidly on him. "My sister thinks I'm a no-good crook," he spat.

Both other men chuckled. "She's not the only one," Slocum said. "If you could be trusted, we'd be having this conversation under much better circumstances."

In the space of a few seconds, Trick lost the color in his face and a cold sweat broke out to dribble down his forehead. "Now that you mention it, I'd like to move this to somewhere that's not so public."

"I just bet you would," Slocum grunted.

"No, seriously. I'm supposed to be dead. I went through a lot of trouble to spread that rumor. I even put on a funeral. Do you know how many folks I had to bribe to do a proper burial without anyone realizing they weren't burying a member of the most influential family in town?" When all he got from Slocum and Duvall were blank stares, Trick added, "A lot. I'm well known around here. All it takes is one person to see me alive and kicking and the news will spread like wildfire. All my work will be for nothing."

Without taking his eyes off Trick, Slocum said, "Take a look around, Duvall. Are we attracting any unwanted attention?"

"Actually," the bounty hunter replied, "there are a few men trying to get a look this way."

Whether Duvall was being truthful or just trying to ruffle Trick's feathers, his words had an immediate effect. The little fellow began squirming so much that it was all Slocum could do to hold him down.

"I can't be seen out here!" Trick whined.

At first glance, Slocum couldn't see the curious folks Duvall had mentioned, but he could sure see the growing anxiety written all over Trick's face. Playing to that, Slocum said, "I don't know. Maybe it'd do folks around here some good to know their favorite son isn't dead."

"Favorite son, my ass," Trick hissed. "If these stingy pricks weren't so fond of poking their noses into my family's affairs, things would run a whole lot smoother. Get me the hell out of plain sight!"

"Hmmm. People making your life miserable by meddling

with your affairs," Slocum mused. "I think I might just know what you mean by that."

If Slocum had ever had doubts about going through so much trouble to follow up on the lies that had put his name upon a reward notice, they were washed away when he saw the panic spreading throughout Trick's entire body. That sight alone made the long ride worthwhile.

"I can pay you," Trick said. "But not a cent if I'm spotted. Jesus, I think Mrs. Randall saw me. That old bitty will spread the word before lunch."

"Really?" Duvall said innocently. Turning toward the street, he waved his hand over his head and shouted, "That you, Mrs. Randall? Awfully late for a stroll, isn't it?"

The reply that came back was barely loud enough to be heard over the passing breeze. "Yes, it is late. I couldn't sleep. Is that Bobby Rose? What are you doin' in the dark?"

"Just passing the time, Mrs. Randall."

"For Christ's sake," Trick snarled in a haggard whisper. "She can't see me here."

"What's it worth to you?" Slocum asked.

"I said I can pay you."

"Bobby?" the old woman asked as she took a few steps toward Duvall.

"Sounds like you're expecting to come into some money," Slocum said. "Or would this be from some bit of change you stole from your own family and stashed away in the event of your pretend death?"

"I didn't steal nothin'."

"Then how would you be able to pay me?"

"Or me?" Duvall asked.

"Who're you talking to, Bobby?" the woman asked. "Are you keeping company with those drunken friends of yours?"

Trick seemed too wound up to get another word out. When he heard the sound of shuffling steps getting closer to him, he turned his face away from the old woman and pressed his head so roughly against the dirt that he practically dug a hole for himself. "I'll be coming into some money soon," he whispered. "The mining company's set to fall into my hands. Since you killed some of my partners, you can have their share. It'll set you both up for years, but not if I don't get the hell out of this old bat's sight!"

Duvall looked over at Slocum, who gave him a single nod. Turning to the old woman, Duvall walked toward her until he was no longer obscured by thick shadows. "Hello, Mrs. Randall. Remember me?"

The old woman stopped, placed a hand over her heart, and immediately shuffled backward. "Oh, my goodness! You're not Bobby Rose."

"No, ma'am," he replied with a warm smile. "My name's Kyle Dunnigan. I'm Jimmy's cousin. Remember Jimmy?"

"Yes," the old woman said hesitantly. "I believe so."

Waving once more, Duvall said, "He sends his best." With that, the bounty hunter turned and walked back toward Slocum and Trick.

The old woman stood still for a moment and studied the trio. Gathering her shawl a bit tighter around her shoulders, she quickly hurried in the opposite direction.

"Who the hell is Jimmy Dunnigan?" Slocum asked.

"Everyone knows a Jimmy something or other."

"Can we get moving now or not?" Trick asked.

Slocum picked the smaller man up by the front of his shirt and hauled him to his feet. The moment Trick was upright, he tried to scamper away. Fortunately, Slocum maintained a tight enough grip to prevent him from going anywhere.

They were in a section of town where the streets were lined with small businesses and a few abandoned storefronts. The place Slocum chose must have been cleaned out by a fire not too long ago because the walls were still coated in ash and the air smelled like soot. He dragged Trick inside and kept going until they reached the back of the building's single room. There was half a staircase leading up to a second floor that was smaller than a toolshed, but none of the men went near it since the entire structure creaked with the promise of falling over.

"All right," Slocum said. "We're out of sight. Finish what you were saying."

"What I was saying?" Trick asked innocently.

Duvall lunged forward to knock the hat off of Trick's head and grab the man by his hair. Compared to his politeness when he'd spoken to the old woman, he now looked like something that had clawed its way up from the pits of hell. "You said we'd be paid!" he snapped. "You said the mining company would be in your hands. Tell us the rest damn quick, before I hollow out your sorry hide and hang it up for this whole fucking town to see!"

"Right, right!" Trick babbled. "I recall now! Yeah. The mining company." He turned to Slocum as if he could no longer bear the sight of Duvall's angry glare. "My whole family don't think highly of me on account of my gambling debts. They think I wouldn't do nothing with the family money apart from running up more debt. I tried to get some money to pay it back and was refused. Can you believe it?"

"Just keep talking," Slocum said.

Trick nodded and continued in a rush of hurried words. "When my granddaddy passed on, he left a piece of the company to all his kin. My parents took a train to California some time ago and left their shares to me, my brothers, and my sister. Over the last few years, my brothers died off, leaving their shares to me and Isabelle. This last spring, I found out that weren't the case. They left all their shares to Isabelle. Not even my own damned brothers trusted me!"

"Imagine that."

"I know!" Trick sighed, without catching a bit of the sarcasm in Slocum's voice. "I knew I wasn't gonna see one bit of the profits so long as everything was being spread out among all us Chestertons. But I know my sister. Isabelle would be content to leave all that money where it was so long as she still had me to front for her interests."

"What's that supposed to mean?" Duvall asked.

In response, Slocum merely shrugged and motioned for

the bounty hunter to shut his mouth so Trick could keep on yapping.

"She and everyone else in my family called me dead-weight," Trick groused. "They thought I was too stupid to know I wouldn't ever see more than a paltry little bit of my family's fortune. I'm the older brother and I should be the one running that company! How the hell could a damn woman run that business better than me?"

"Seems like that woman's running it pretty well," Slocum said. "She even managed to find time to bring her brother's killer to justice."

Trick's mouth tightened into an aggravated line. "She wasn't supposed to do all that. The last thing I wanted was a bunch of bounty hunters sniffing around. All I needed was for her to do what I knew she would do."

"Which is?"

"Pull all the mining company shares together, nice and legal. According to my sources, that's just what she done!" Trick proudly announced. "She's got all the papers together, so I can finally come in and take what's mine."

"Wait a second," Slocum said. "You faked your own death just to force your sister to consolidate the family business?"

"While I was alive, I was just holding on to a bunch of odds and ends that was hardly worth anything on their own. Now that I'm supposed to be dead, every last bit of it goes to Isabelle. Now that she's at the head of the table, I can take her out of the picture, swoop in, and claim it all for myself as the last legal Chesterton to show up on all those deeds and whatnot."

"You think she'll just give it up?" Duvall asked.

"She'd better. Otherwise, she can take my place in that box that was buried outside of town."

Slocum glared at Trick as if he meant to burn a set of holes through the smaller man's head. "You'd kill your own sister?"

"It won't come to that!" Trick sputtered. "All I need is to get my hands on the papers she collected from all the safes, banks, and lawyers from around the country. She's been doing it since the funeral because there ain't nobody left to hold the odds and ends anymore. Also, there was some money tied up in accounts or funds or whatever that wouldn't be freed until I died. Now that it's happened, she pulled all that together, too! There's more money in the company safe now than when I was workin' there!"

Duvall chuckled and shook his head. "It sounds to me like you don't even understand how a business works. Do you even realize all the rules, regulations, and details that go into managing large sums of money?"

Judging by the expression on Trick's face, he didn't even follow Duvall's question all the way through to the end. Finally, he just grunted, "My sister is the only Chesterton left with any ownership in that company, and when she hands it over, it'll all belong to *me*."

"But you're dead," Slocum pointed out. "At least, as far as the law's concerned."

"The law can be twisted around a lot of ways." Nodding and winking in a most obnoxious manner, Trick added, "I got that angle covered. Someone's already in a perfect spot to tell me when the perfect time is to make my grand entrance. It'll just be another time when a fellow got lost and folks thought he was dead. Once I show up, it ain't like anyone can say I'm dead. That happens all the time, right? When I come back into my company, my sister will be the one to disappear. My man inside the company is so close to her that he'll steer her right off the face of the earth when I tell him to. After I claim what's rightfully mine, there won't be anything anyone can do about it." Before Trick could get too pleased with himself, he caught the brunt of both sets of intent stares being aimed at him.

"Or," Trick said, "I could just get all the company shares together and sell them to the highest bidder. That'd be a lot quicker. If you let me see this through, I'll see to it you get a good cut from that sale. There's enough cash being kept right in the company safe to make you men rich. Let me work my magic and I'll line your pockets."

"You hardly have the brains God gave a mule," Slocum said. "Not only is this plan stupid, but it's more despicable than walking into that mining company and robbing it. Hell, at least a robbery takes some sand and a bit of planning. All you're doing is putting your sister through hell and then waiting for her to look the other way so you can pick her pockets. You've barely even thought the whole thing through! Your family probably never trusted you with any money because you're a damned idiot!"

"That's a little harsh," Trick grumbled.

"Says the man who set up his own bullshit funeral," Duvall pointed out with a chuckle.

Shrugging as if he was ridding himself of his own conscience, Trick said, "Let me see my plan through and I'll make it worth both your whiles. I just need to have a word with Jervis."

"He's the one that's been spying on your sister?" Duvall asked.

Trick nodded. "Yep. He's the only one of my men to get close enough to see part of the combination when she opened her safe. The way he's been working on her lately, he may even be closer by now!"

17

By nine o'clock the next morning, Jervis had been working on Isabelle Chesterton for the better part of an hour. She sat perched on the edge of her desk with her legs spread and him standing directly between them. Gripping the edge of the desk with both hands, she leaned back and savored the feel of him sliding in and out of her. Slowly, she shook her head to allow her blond hair to tumble down her back.

"Just like that," she purred. "Nice and slow."

Jervis's shirt was unbuttoned down to his waist and his britches were gathered around his boots. Rubbing his hands along the taut muscles of her thighs, he looked down to watch his stiff cock part the golden, downy hair between her legs. She was wet and warm down there. Whenever he plunged all the way inside, she pushed a contented groan up from the back of her throat. It was an effort to keep his pace steady, but he did what she told him to do.

When Jervis reached up to grab her breast, Isabelle stopped him by pressing her hand over his. "Don't rumple my dress too much. I need to look presentable."

"Presentable?" Jervis asked as he looked down at her exposed thighs and glistening pussy. "I'll show you presentable." The sight of her made him grow even harder and he reached around to cup her tight little ass in both hands. The moment he saw she was about to scold him again, Jervis pulled her as close to the edge of the desk as possible and thrust in and out of her with fast, powerful strokes.

Isabelle grabbed his shoulder with one hand and leaned back while using her other hand to brace herself against the top of the desk. Pumping her hips in time to his rhythm, she grunted, "You should obey my orders, mister. Otherwise, you'll be disciplined."

"I like the sound of that."

Suddenly, Isabelle placed a hand flat on his chest and pushed him away. "Watch your tone with me," she snarled. "I'm the owner of this company. Don't forget that. Step back."

Jervis stepped back and watched her climb down from the desk. From the waist up, she looked only slightly rumpled after a meeting with the company managers earlier that morning. Below the waist, however, her skirts were bunched up to show a trim body and privates that were slick from their lovemaking. Her legs were so long that she didn't need to step down too far for her boots to touch the floor. The upper portions of those boots were still laced up to just below her knee.

Turning around, she looked back at him over her shoulder and then hiked her skirts up to show her rounded little rump. "You know what to do from here?" she asked.

Jervis quickly nodded. "Yes, ma'am."

"Then get to work."

He placed his hands on her hips and moved in behind her. Isabelle knew when to arch her back and just how high to lift her heels off the floor to accommodate him. His cock slid into her as if it had been molded to fit into that spot. Both of them let out long breaths as he eased into her as far as he could go.

Isabelle leaned forward and rested her arms on the desk. As Jervis built up speed, she allowed his movements to rock her as well as the desk until the wooden legs creaked. Soon, he thrust into her faster and harder. Isabelle smiled and allowed her entire body to move back and forth, bumping against him so his thrusts penetrated with even more force.

"Stand up straight," she said. "Just like I told you."

Like any man, Jervis didn't take kindly to being bossed around by a woman. Seeing her snap her head around to glare at him, however, was something that he liked very much indeed.

"Do it!" she snapped. "Like I told you."

He straightened his back and stood up straighter, which slightly adjusted the angle at which he entered her. The smooth surface of his rigid pole brushed against a spot inside her that caused Isabelle to press her hands firmly against the desk and tremble ever so slightly.

"Yes," she purred. "That's the spot."

Jervis stayed in that position, pumping in and out of her so he hit that same spot every time. Right when he could tell she was about to climax, he stopped.

"What are you doing?" she demanded.

"Whatever the hell I want to," he replied.

She nodded just as he tightened his grip on her and buried his stiff cock all the way in her. He hit the sweet spot so hard that he stole the breath right out of Isabelle's lungs. As he continued to drive into her, she could only bite her lip and make little contented grunts. Any louder, and she knew she'd attract attention from the other offices.

Smirking, Jervis waited for the trembles again, and then slapped his hand flat against the side of her ass. Isabelle's orgasm was powerful enough, but that slap pushed her even further over the edge. She let out a breathy moan and then quickly clenched her mouth shut. Before her trembling had subsided, someone knocked on the door.

"Everything all right in there?" one of her aides asked from outside the office.

In the best semblance of a normal voice that she could muster, Isabelle replied, "Yes, I just stubbed my toe."

"Need any help?"

"No. I'm fine. Just . . ." Sucking in a breath as Jervis eased back, she could only exhale once he'd slid fully out of her. "Just go tend to the claims I told you about this morning."

"Yes, ma'am." Then Jervis asked. "You like hearing men take orders from you?"

She nodded and turned around to face him. "You know I do."

"Well, it's your turn to take orders from me."

Her eyes widened and she pulled in a quick, excited breath. "What do you want me to do?"

After taking a step back from her, Jervis said, "Get on your knees."

Isabelle smiled and lowered herself to both knees in front of him. From there, she cupped him in one hand and wrapped her lips around the tip of his cock. She moved her head back and forth, rubbing her lips against every inch of his shaft. When she felt his hands rest on her head to guide her, Isabelle began flicking her tongue on the underside of his shaft.

Jervis might have been talking tough a few seconds ago, but she quickly took the reins back from him. Once she found a good rhythm and began moving her tongue for good measure, she nearly brought him to his knees. Isabelle smiled as she continued to suck him. When she felt his pole become even more rigid in her mouth, she made a soft, appreciative sound in the back of her throat. The hum of that sound pushed Jervis past his limit and he exploded in her mouth.

She swallowed every last drop that he gave her, and then calmly stood back up again. Dabbing at her lips with a handkerchief, she said, "Get dressed and get out of my office. I can't have anyone suspicious about what's going on in here."

"What if I happened to let it slip?" he asked while buckling his belt.

"Then you'd be out of a job and unable to find work in this company, this town, or even this territory. Honestly,

Jervis. You've got talents, but not nearly enough to try and threaten me with some sort of scandal. Most men around here just think I'm only in this office because of my family. They'd probably think more harshly of you for taking orders from me."

Jervis smirked and nodded. "I was just foolin'," he lied.

"Sure you were. Now get to work."

He had plenty he wanted to say, but kept it all to himself until he was dressed and out of Isabelle's office. Even after her door was closed, he only grumbled under his breath so there was no chance of being heard by any of the guards posted along the hallway. Once he got down the stairs to the second floor, Jervis stopped.

He looked up and down the hall, only to find one man leaning against the railing at the top of the staircase. As he walked down the hall, Jervis peeked into the other rooms along the way. Most of the offices were supposed to be occupied by the company's higher-paid accountants, but the rooms he was most interested in were empty.

Once Jervis reached the stairs, he looked over at the man standing there and asked, "Where is everyone?"

The man was burly and wore a suit that wasn't as expensive as one of Isabelle Chesterton's dresses, but was a bit fancier than the tattered rags covering the backs of the miners doing business in the building. He looked down to survey the modest amount of bartering going on downstairs, which was fairly typical for that time of day. "What do you mean?" he grunted.

"The guards! Tad, Mackie, Harold, Chavez, any of them. Where the hell are they?"

The other man shrugged. "I figured they were in town somewhere making their rounds."

"What rounds?"

"They don't answer to me," the man in the suit declared. "They strut around without answering to anyone. Hell, they're practically the law around here. How would I know where they went?"

"Have you seen any of them since all that shooting last night?"

The man shook his head. "They were the ones that would look in on something like that. I warned Miss Chesterton against letting those men do so much around here, but nobody listens to me."

Jervis wasn't listening to him either. Instead, he hurried down the stairs and rushed toward the front door. Along the way, he passed several miners, landowners, and other folks without recognizing one familiar face. One of those faces recognized him, however, and the man behind that face reached out to snag Jervis's sleeve.

"Let go of me, tin-panner," Jervis grunted as he tried to pull loose.

The man who'd grabbed him might have been short, but his grip was strong enough to keep Jervis from getting away. When he had Jervis's full attention, the man pulled down the bandanna that covered a good portion of his chin. Thanks to the high collar of his jacket and the big hat pulled down to his eyebrows, Patrick Chesterton had been able to walk into the mining company without being spotted.

"Where the hell have you been?" Trick asked.

Jervis still squinted at the smaller man. "That you, Pat?"

Trick bared his teeth and silently hissed for Jervis to stop using his name. He also inadvertently kept Jervis's attention long enough for two other men to sidle up on either side of him.

"Mornin'," Slocum said as he stuck his Colt against Jervis's midsection so it was mostly hidden from view.

When Jervis turned away from Slocum, he was immediately confronted by Duvall. The bounty hunter smiled amiably and took the gun from Jervis's holster.

Looking at Trick, Jervis asked, "Where's everyone else?"

"Tad's bein' seen to by Doc Shaver and the rest are dead," Trick replied. "Didn't you hear the shooting?"

"All right," Slocum said. "You two can catch up on old times later. Right now, we've got some business to conduct.

Escort us up to Miss Chesterton's office and be real calm about it. You make one move I don't like, and I'll drop you right in front of all these workingmen."

Duvall took in his surroundings like a hawk surveying a canyon floor. "There doesn't seem to be many gunmen left around here."

Smirking while glaring at Jervis, Slocum said, "Then we should be able to clean out this whole place and walk away free and clear."

"I'll take you upstairs," Jervis growled.

As Duvall prodded him to start walking toward the stairs, Trick snarled, "There's no reason for this. You're both throwing away a fortune."

"Maybe. Maybe not." Turning to the bounty hunter, Slocum said, "You stay here and I'll have a word with Miss Chesterton."

Duvall's eyes narrowed as he asked, "You're bargaining without me present?"

"You're the one holding our ace. Wait for my signal and play our hand. If I don't come back, you've still got one hell of a bargaining chip to hand over to a rich family."

Reluctantly, Duvall nodded.

Slocum nudged Jervis so both men could climb the stairs. By the time they got to the third floor, they hadn't found anyone standing in their way. Even the man in the suit had found something else to do. After knocking on Isabelle's door a few times, Slocum used Jervis to push it open.

"What's the meaning of this?" Isabelle asked as she stood up behind her desk.

"This man's got a gun!" Jervis shouted as he struggled to pull away from his escort.

Slocum let Jervis go and eased his Colt back into its holster. "Just give me a moment and I can explain myself."

"Someone shoot this man!" Jervis wailed.

Isabelle looked around as if she was trying to find the army her employee was trying to muster. Finally, she asked, "What's going on here? Where are my guards?"

"My name's John Slocum. I came to see to it that the reward you're offering for my scalp is taken back."

"You're John Slocum?" she asked as she reached into one of her desk drawers to remove a small .32. "Give me one reason why I shouldn't kill you for what you did to my brother!"

"How about if I prove I didn't kill your brother?"

"How would you do something like that?"

"Care to follow me?"

Reluctantly, Isabelle walked around her desk. She kept her pistol in front of her so it was aimed at Slocum every step of the way.

"Hand me that gun," Jervis demanded. "I'll deal with this killer!"

"Disarm Mr. Slocum," she said.

"Gladly."

Slocum didn't like having his gun taken from him, but he had a holdout pistol tucked away where he could get to it in a pinch. More than likely, he would draw that holdout if Jervis tried searching for more than just the Colt Navy, but it didn't come to that. As soon as Jervis took the Colt, Isabelle said, "Give me that gun."

"What?" Jervis protested. "I won't be able to watch your back if I'm not armed."

"Watch my back?" she scoffed. "The only time you ever watched my back is when you were admiring it. Hand me that gun and do it now."

"You don't know what you're doing."

Thumbing back the hammer of her .32, she pointed it at Jervis and said, "You and every other manager in this company thinks that very same thing. That's why every decision I make is questioned or disobeyed. You think I'm blind as well as deaf and stupid? Do you think you and all your guards strut around this town like you own it without me knowing every last thing you men do?"

"That's just to protect your interests," Jervis said. "Just like we—"

"If you try telling me you protect this town, I'll shoot you right through your lying mouth. There are only a few things you do well," she added. "Don't insult my intelligence by trying to convince me you know a damn thing about anything else."

Jervis knew when to keep his mouth shut, but he obviously wasn't happy about it. He grudgingly tossed the Colt Navy onto Isabelle's desk and then crossed his arms like a petulant child.

"As for you, Mr. Slocum, make your case quickly. I've got no problem with killing you myself and saving my company fifteen thousand dollars."

Despite the fact that he was being held at gunpoint, Slocum grinned. "What I've got to show you is right downstairs," he said.

"Let's go."

When it became clear that she intended to hear Slocum out, Jervis dove for the Colt lying on the desk. Isabelle jumped back in surprise and twitched her finger on the trigger of her .32. Her shot was well off its mark, but it distracted Jervis long enough for him to be blindsided by Slocum.

Slocum rushed at Jervis, wrapped one arm around his neck, and used the other hand to slam Jervis's face against the desk. While Jervis wobbled unsteadily on his feet, Slocum swept his legs out from under him. Jervis hit against the side of the desk on his way to the floor and flopped onto his back.

"Enough!" Isabelle said. Holding her .32 in a shaky hand, she watched as the man in the cheap suit rushed to her door. "Where are the rest of my guards?"

"I thought they were—"

"Never mind," she snapped, cutting off the man in the suit as if she already knew what he was going to say.

Rather than reach for his holdout weapon, Slocum kept his hands up where Isabelle could see them. "Care to see what I brought you?"

"Might as well."

The man in the suit stumbled down the hall, flummoxed by what was going on. When they reached the top of the stairs from the second to the first floor, it became all too clear that he wasn't the only one feeling that way. Everyone on the first floor was either staring up at them or trying to hide under a desk.

Isabelle pressed the barrel of her .32 against Slocum's shoulder blade. "It's all right, everyone!" she announced from the top of the stairs. "Nothing to worry about."

Slocum looked straight down at Duvall and gave him a single, pronounced nod.

"Well, lookee here!" Duvall said while turning toward Trick as if the smaller man had appeared amid a puff of smoke. "Is that Patrick Chesterton?" The bounty hunter pulled off Trick's oversized hat and then yanked the bandanna from around his neck. "Why, it sure is!"

Many of the miners still looked confused, but some of them, along with all of the company accountants and surveyors, looked positively amazed.

"Patrick?" Isabelle gasped. "Is that really you?"

"Yeah. Uhhh. . .I'm back!"

But she wasn't about to get swept up in the tearful reunion that Trick was trying to instigate. "Where have you been, Patrick?"

"Last thing I recall, I fell off my horse and hit my head." Rubbing his head for effect, Trick winced and asked, "How long have I been out?"

Isabelle still wasn't impressed. "There was a funeral. Your funeral."

"That must have been some poor fool who—"

"Who Jervis and half a dozen others on the payroll swore was you."

The astonishment in Trick's voice was almost believable when he insisted, "Then they were lying! See for yourself."

"I've heard rumors that you were alive," Isabelle said as she slowly made her way down the stairs. "When I went to square away your debt with one of those gambling halls you frequented, I heard that you'd been seen in a cabin outside of town."

Trick's eyebrows perked up when he asked, "So you squared away my debt?"

"No," Isabelle sternly replied. "When I heard that you were seen sneaking in to get whiskey and visit a whore, I lost my charitable impulse."

"You heard what? That's preposterous!"

"Is it?" Forcing Slocum to walk down with her to one of the bottom steps, she looked around at everyone else in the room and asked, "Has anyone else heard rumors like that?"

"These people don't know me!" Trick growled. He started to say something else, but Duvall reined him in.

"I don't need specifics," Isabelle continued. "Just a show of hands as to who among you has heard that my brother was alive and sneaking about."

At first, there was silence.

Then, one of the miners stuck his hand up.

Within a few seconds, a few more miners raised their hands. A few seconds after that, some of the company managers and surveyors followed suit.

"Aw, what the hell do they know?" Trick snapped.

"Apparently," Isabelle said, "they know my brother just as well as I always did."

Trick pulled his arm out of Duvall's grasp and stomped toward the stairs as though he didn't care about getting shot or taken down. "Yeah? Well, you and all of these assholes can go to hell! I'm alive and I'm back. This is still my family's business and I intend on reclaiming everything I'm owed. In fact, I intend on taking *all* of it away from you." He glared at Isabelle. "You wanna sling rumors? I know you've been fucking one of your own employees! If any of our partners or associates had a problem with a woman sitting up in that office, they'll sure know their doubts are well founded now!"

The only reaction Isabelle showed was a flicker of sadness in her eyes, which was quickly replaced by the tired determination that comes from fighting a hard yet familiar battle for a very long time. "I'll fight to keep my company, Patrick. If you want to discuss this, let's do so in private."

"No," Trick said as Duvall came behind him to grab his shoulder. "Let's do it right here in front of witnesses. Legal matters are best when there are witnesses. You want to fight? I'll fight. That is, unless you'd rather buy me out with a nice, healthy percentage tacked onto the value of my shares."

Isabelle sighed and bowed her head.

"Excuse me," Slocum said. "I think I may be of some use here."

"You've done plenty, Mr. Slocum," Isabelle sighed. "I've got a lot to tend to right now, but I'll see to it that the reward I offered for your capture is rescinded. I'm sorry you had to go through all of this, but I can handle my brother from here on."

"And what about all the hell he's going to put you through with contracts, legal claims, and all that sort of nonsense?"

"Unless you know your way around a courtroom," Isabelle sighed, "I can't think of what I would need you for."

"I'm no lawyer, but a friend of mine in the Montana Territory knows one. Have you ever heard of Daniel Reavorly?"

Suddenly, Isabelle's eyes brightened. "The Terror of Sacramento? You can get him to help me?"

"I'll be heading back to McKalb to let that friend of mine know I'm still in one piece. I can do my best to put Daniel on your case if you'd be willing to pay a small finder's fee."

"Don't you mean referral fee?" Isabelle asked.

"Hey!" Trick yapped. "Don't talk like I ain't here no more!"

Continuing as if the smaller man wasn't there, Slocum said, "There's the referral plus the finder's fee for sniffing out your brother. You'd be real interested to know everything he had in store for you and your family."

"Yes, Mr. Slocum," she said. "I believe I would."

18

Sheriff White pushed open the door to his office and stepped outside. "How about I split a bottle with you, Sheriff?" Slocum offered as he emerged from the office behind him.

The lawman scowled and said, "For what you put me and my deputies through, I should insist on a lot more than that."

"A bottle for each of you then. That, on top of the time I just served, ought to be enough."

Tossing the Colt Navy at Slocum, the sheriff said, "That's more like it."

Slocum caught his weapon, and then threw the sheriff a wave before walking away. Leaning against a post across the street, Duvall shook his head.

"What's got you looking so smug?" Slocum asked as he joined him.

"Out of jail after only a few weeks? How'd you manage that one?"

"The sheriff admitted he was wrong for tossing me in there, and I did break an ordinance or two, so we worked out

185

an arrangement. I needed to bide my time while Daniel sifted through all that legal bullshit anyway."

"Beats getting hung or hunted, I suppose."

Slocum shrugged his shoulders and rubbed a sore spot at the back of his neck. "Once I got used to the smell, it wasn't so bad. Fixing up the hole I made kept me busy for a while. How are things in Shackley?"

Stooping down to pick up a leather satchel, the bounty hunter handed it over and said, "See for yourself."

Opening the satchel, Slocum rummaged through several bundles of cash and let out a low whistle. "Is this all my share?"

"No. That's the whole sum Isabelle Chesterton paid us. I figured we'd count it together and split it up."

"You trusted me enough to bring this all the way back here?" Slocum asked with a scowl.

"I've heard about you, Slocum. You could have made things turn out a lot bloodier than they did."

"You mean I could have shot you and been done with it."

"You could have tried." Duvall chuckled. "Anyway, I did shoot at you first, so I figure the least I could do to make up for it was treat you like a real partner."

Slocum nodded and said, "That goes a long way with me. Still, you didn't have to come all the way out here to see me turned loose."

"I've been here for a little while already. Trick's such an idiot that he hired on some crooked lawyers to try and fleece his sister as soon as possible. All any of them could do against the Terror of Sacramento was lie down and pray for a quick death. Isabelle paid us that reward plus a ten-thousand-dollar bonus for a job well done."

"Ten thousand more?"

Duvall nodded. "She's set to take over that company lock, stock, and barrel. I was going to ask for five thousand, but she was so happy to put Trick in his place that she made an even more generous offer right away. If you want to argue for more, be my guest."

Slocum studied the bounty hunter and felt the weight of the satchel. His instinct told him there was more than likely around twenty-five thousand in there. Another set of instincts told him that any bounty hunter would more than likely take a stab at squeezing a rich lady for even more money, and then lie about the true amount to a partner that had been serving a few easy weeks in a piss-hole jail.

"Fine," Slocum said as he led the way to The Wheelhouse Hotel. "Let's split this up so I can treat myself to a good bed and an even better woman."

If Duvall had pocketed some extra money, Slocum figured the bounty hunter had earned it by doing the back-and-forth work over the last month. Besides, considering how much of a return he'd gotten the last time he'd helped Nellie build her hotels, Slocum knew he could invest whatever his share might be and still ride away with some very full pockets. Of course, it would be a while before Nellie would let Slocum leave his room.

Watch for

**SLOCUM AND THE FOUR PEAKS
RANGE WAR**

370th novel in the exciting SLOCUM series
from Jove

Coming in December!